INSPIRING LEGENDS AND TALES
WITH A MORAL II

Stories From Around the World

Emerson Klees

The Human Values Series
Cameo Press, Rochester, New York

The Human Values Series

Role Models of Human Values

One Plus One Equals Three—Pairing Man / Woman Strengths:
  Role Models of Teamwork (1998)
Entrepreneurs in History—Success vs. Failure:
  Entrepreneurial Role Models (1999)
Staying With It: Role Models of Perseverance (1999)
The Drive to Succeed: Role Models of Motivation (2002)
The Will to Stay With It: Role Models of Determination (2002)

The Moral Navigator

Inspiring Legends and Tales With a Moral I: Stories From
  Around the World (2007)
Inspiring Legends and Tales With a Moral II: Stories From
  Around the World (2007)
Inspiring Legends and Tales With a Moral III: Stories From
  Around the World (2007)

Copyright © 2007 by Emerson C. Klees

Cameo Press
P. O. Box 18131
Rochester, New York 14618

Library of Congress Control Number: 2007905079

ISBN 1-891046-19-5

Printed in the United States of America
9 8 7 6 5 4 3 2 1

Preface

A moral conveys the ethical significance or practical lesson to be learned from a story. It is the principle taught by a legend or tale that portrays what is right or just. What we learn from stories with a moral is of a general or strategic nature rather than a detailed or tactical one. A moral provides a background against which to measure our attitude and behavior. The moral of a well-told story can inspire us by highlighting a virtue to emulate.

The human qualities illustrated in these legends and tales include compassion, courage, determination, humility, loyalty, perseverance, resourcefulness, and unselfishness. Some of them are familiar, such as those about Daniel, King Arthur, and Samson; most are not as well known. The less familiar ones also deserve our attention. These stories uplift as well as entertain and show that our potential is greater than we think.

TABLE OF CONTENTS

Page No.

Introduction   6

*I*MMORTAL / ENDURING   *Chapter 1*   8
   The Round Table of King Arthur   9
   The Legend of Samson   11
   The Golden Touch of King Midas   17
   Daniel and the Fiery Furnace   19
   St. George and the Dragon   21

*N*OTABLE / LOYAL   *Chapter 2*   25
   Androcles and the Lion   26
   Daniel in the Lions' Den   27
   The Three Questions   29
   Icarus and Daedalus   33
   The Legend of the Minotaur   35

*S*ELF-DETERMINED / RESPONSIBLE   *Chapter 3*   40
   The Tale of Sulayman Bey   41
   The Maiden and the Morning Star   42
   The Diamond Necklace   43
   The Legend of the Peace Queen   47
   The Legend of Three Beautiful Princesses   49

*P*ERSEVERING / RESOURCEFUL   *Chapter 4*   58
   Tamerlane and the Ant   59
   From Each According to His Ability   60
   The Old Man and the Gold Crowns   63
   A Message to Garcia   65
   Mammon and the Archer   68

*I*NDEFATIGABLE / UNSELFISH   *Chapter 5*   73
   The Salamanna Grapes   74
   The Clown of God   76
   The Indian Cinderella   81
   A New York Merchant's Way to Wealth   83
   The Gift of the Magi   85

Page No.

*R*ESOLUTE / *COURAGEOUS*   *Chapter 6*   90
     Citizen William Tell   91
     The Bravery of Arnold von Winkelried   95
     The Legend of the Arabian Astrologer   99
     The Legend of the Spirits' Mountain   108
     The Cave of the Moor's Daughter   114

*E*MPATHETIC / *COMPASSIONATE*   *Chapter 7*   118
     The Lover of People   119
     Work, Death, and Sickness   121
     The Rich Brother and the Poor Brother   123
     The House in the Wood   129
     The Piece of String   133

*S*PECIAL / *MEMORABLE*   *Chapter 8*   138
     The Open French Doors   139
     For Want of a Horseshoe Nail   141
     The Lady, or the Tiger   143
     Tom Sawyer Gives Up the Brush   147
     The Last Leaf   150

Epilogue   155

Bibliography   157

Introduction

A legend is a story or narrative, with some historical basis, often unverifiable, handed down from generation to generation. Much of its content may be fiction, but it has some basis in fact. A legend is usually about people who actually lived, places that really existed, or events that in fact occurred, all embedded in details added later in subsequent retellings

Legends are considered authentic in the society in which they originated. Frequently, it is difficult to determine the boundary between fact and fiction. Folktales, initially handed down by word of mouth, are not considered historically factual. However, the theme of a folktale may appear in a legend or in time turn into a legend. The boundary between legends and folktales is not well defined.

The distinction between legends and myths is described by Richard Cavendish in the introduction to *Legends of the World*:

> Legends are on a different plane from myths, which are imaginative traditions about the nature and destiny of the world, the gods, and the human race. In some cases, as in the Bible, a people's account of the past begins with myth—the creation of the world—and then shades over into legends about the founding figures and leaders of the nation in its early history. Legends are set on the human rather than the divine level, and the central characters of legends are human beings, not gods, although they are often larger-than-life human beings with supernatural powers.

Legends become part of an inherited body of beliefs and values that identify a society. These stories provide insight into the societies that created them. Often legends are passed on to subsequent generations by storytellers.

Many parallels exist among the legends of the world. For example, similarities exist in many stories of the supernatural birth of heroes, including those in which one or both parents were gods. Other similarities are found in the dangers that confronted many of the heroes of legends as children. In the Greek legend of the

Pleiades, for example, the seven daughters of Atlas were changed into stars. In a parallel Iroquois Indian legend, seven young Indian children became a constellation called Oot-kwa-tah by the Iroquois.

These legends and tales are inspiring. They remind us that our lives do not necessarily have to be small lives, and that if we reach out, we can achieve much more than our perceived limitations allow us. These stories not only teach us about moral values, they provide us with examples of behavior to emulate or in some cases to avoid, and they elevate our attitude towards life.

Chapter 1

IMMORTAL / ENDURING

To achieve great things we must live as though
we were never going to die.

Marquis de Vauvenargues, *Reflections and Maxims*

The Round Table of King Arthur

With the decline of Roman power during the sixth century when Rome called legions home for her own defense, the countries of northern Europe were virtually left without national governments. Regional chiefs held power to the extent that each could enforce his will in his domain. Occasionally, they would unite for common interest; more often they were hostile to one another. The poorer classes were at the mercy of the powerful. Without some restraint of power of the chiefs, society would have lapsed into barbarism.

Several restraints existed. First were the rivalries between the chiefs themselves, whose mutual jealousies built in restraints. Second, the influence of the church, whether for pure or selfish reasons, interposed to protect the weak. Also, a generosity and sense of right, however much influenced by passion and selfishness, dwelt naturally in the heart of man. From this source sprang chivalry, which presented an ideal of the heroic character combining invincible strength, valor, justice, modesty, loyalty, courtesy, compassion, and devotion to the church. Even if people did not achieve this ideal in real life, it provided a model to emulate.

Leading up to the reign of King Arthur, the most powerful of the local British kings was Vortigern, who ruled from Wales to southeast Britain. In 425, Vortigern had four adversaries: the Picts in the north; the Scots, who invaded from bases in Wales; the Saxons, a constant menace on the southeast coast; and a contingent of Romano-British, who wanted to restore Roman-inspired authority. Threatened by four enemies, Vortigern decided to fight three of them by making a pact with the fourth, the Saxons, to whom he gave land in return for military support.

Vortigern was defeated by Arthur's father, Uther, and his uncle, Pendragon. Pendragon assumed the throne but was killed in a subsequent battle with the Saxons. Uther became king and used his brother's name, Pendragon, as the title of the elective sovereign.

King Arthur was a prince of the tribe of Britons called Silures, who were from South Wales. Arthur was only fifteen in 510, when he was elected to succeed his father as king at a general meeting of nobles. His election was not without opposition; many ambitious competitors sought the throne. Although Arthur was elected, his coronation was delayed.

A stone in which a sword called Excalibur was firmly fixed was found outside the local church door. Bishop Brice announced that whoever could draw the sword out of the stone would be acknowledged as sovereign of the Britons. The famous knights all tried to pull it out and failed.

At the annual tournament, Arthur assisted his foster brother, Sir Kay, in the lists. Sir Kay fought with great valor but broke his sword. Arthur went to Sir Kay's home for a replacement but no one was there. Returning to the tournament, Arthur passed by the church and saw the sword sticking out of the stone. He pulled it out with ease and took it to Sir Kay. To confirm the doubters, the sword was replaced in the stone, and Sir Kay attempted unsuccessfully to draw it out. Again, Arthur was the only one who could withdraw it. This sign confirmed that Arthur was the rightful king, and a day was set for his coronation.

Immediately after his coronation, King Arthur was confronted by eleven kings and one duke, who were encamped in Rockingham Forest with a substantial army. With the help of King Ban and King Bohort from Brittany, he defeated the rebel kings. Next he took the field against the Saxons. King Arthur won twelve victories over the Saxons. The most important of them was the final battle at Badon in 518, which was so decisive that Arthur had no further trouble from them.

During Arthur's lifetime, the Saxon advance from southeast to southwest was checked. According to legend, King Arthur carried the cross of the Lord on his shoulders for three days and three nights during the Battle of Badon. Some historians think that the cross was emblazoned on his shield.

King Arthur fought to defend the lands of his ally, King Leodegrance, against King Ryence of North Wales. He met Princess Guinevere, daughter of King Leodegrance, and subsequently married her. The Arthurian legend was embellished over the centuries with places like Camelot and with knights such as Galahad, Gawain, and Lancelot.

One of King Arthur's principal accomplishments in addition to being an advocate of chivalry was the establishment of a conference of kings who worked together to confront mutual enemies. Their conferences were held at the round table, which had originally been made by Arthur's nephew, Merlin the magician, for King Uther.

The size of the round table varied widely in legend. Although it has been described as small as having places for twelve, it usually was described as accommodating one hundred and fifty. According to legend, one seat, called the Siege Perilous, was left vacant for the best knight in the world. The only knight who tried sitting in it disappeared and was never seen again.

In addition to the Battle of Badon, the other documented battle of King Arthur was the Battle of Camlann in Cornwall in 542. King Arthur was mortally wounded and was conveyed to the sea near Glastonbury, where he died and was buried. Another version of the Arthurian legend relates that Arthur did not die but was carried off and healed of his wounds, thus allowing for his reappearance to avenge his countrymen and to reinstate them in the sovereignty of Britain.

Moral: As displayed by chivalry, generosity and a sense of right exist in the heart of man. When the need for acting in concert for the common good occurs, a responsible leader will emerge.

Adapted from: Thomas Bulfinch, "The Age of Chivalry," *Bulfinch's Mythology*, and Elizabeth Jenkins, "Fact and Legend," *The Mystery of Arthur*

The Legend of Samson

In the eleventh century BC, there was not yet a king in Israel, nor any central authority. The neighboring nations, including Canaan and Philistia, took advantage of the weak Hebrew tribes to launch campaigns of conquest and pillage against them. Occasionally, a leader, such as Gideon, would emerge to lead his tribe and sometimes several tribes into retaliatory battle. If he won, he would become the shofet, the leader and judge. The Israelites swung back and forth between periods of oppression and redemption, as related in the Book of Judges.

During this turbulent time over three thousand years ago lived a man and a woman of the tribe of Dan. They lived in Zorah in the Judean lowlands, a particularly volatile region on the boundary between Israel and Philistia. For the Philistines, taking Zorah was the first step in conquering the Judean hill country. The man's name was Manoah; the woman's name is not known. She had borne no children.

One day when the woman was alone, an angel of God appeared before her and told her that she would conceive and bear a son. The angel also gave her instructions and some good news: "Be careful not to drink wine or other intoxicant, or to eat anything unclean; for you are going to conceive and bear a son; let no razor touch his hair, for the boy is to be a Nazirite to God from the womb on. It is he who will begin to deliver Israel from the Philistines." Among the ancient Hebrews, a Nazirite was one who took certain vows of abstinence, particularly from drinking wine and from cutting one's hair.

The woman told her husband what the stranger had said, and that he was frightening and had looked like an angel of God. She admitted that she had not asked where he was from or what his name was. Manoah prayed to God for further guidance. He asked for the angel of God to come again and tell them how to act with the boy who was to be born. The angel returned for a second visit and Manoah asked him if he were the one who had visited his wife. The angel replied that he was. Manoah said that he hoped the angel's word would come true and asked what rules should be observed for the boy. The angel reiterated everything he had said before.

Manoah invited the angel to stay while he prepared a young goat for him to eat. The angel suggested that Manoah sacrifice the kid to God, not to him. Manoah asked the angel's name and was told that it was unknowable. Manoah placed the meal offering on a rock. The angel produced fire from the rock and ascended through the flames into heaven. Manoah was convinced that he had indeed seen an angel of God.

The wife of Manoah gave birth to Samson, which in Hebrew means "little sun." As he grew, the Lord blessed him and said: "The spirit of the Lord began to move him in the encampment of Dan, between Zorah and Eshtaol." When Samson was a young man, he traveled to Timnah. While visiting, he noticed a young woman among the Philistines to whom he was attracted. When he returned to Zorah, he asked his parents to obtain the young woman for him as a wife. They asked why he did not choose a wife from their own people. Why did he have to take his wife from the Philistines, their longtime enemy? Samson insisted that she was "the right woman" for him.

Samson and his father and mother set out from Zorah to Timnah to visit the young woman. On a hilltop at the crest of the Zorah ridge, Samson's parents rested to catch their breath. He wandered off toward the entrance to the vineyards of Timnah and was attacked by a lion. Without hesitating, he tore the lion apart with his bare hands. When he rejoined his mother and father, he did not tell them about what he had done.

When they arrived in Timnah, Samson again met the young woman and confirmed that she was "the right one" and observed his parents' reaction to her. They returned home, and when he traveled back to Timnah to marry the woman, he detoured from his path to see the remains of the lion. As he stood before the dead lion, he saw a swarm of bees in the lion's skeleton. He bent down and scooped honey into his hand. He ate the honey as he walked toward Timnah.

The Philistines chose thirty companions to accompany Samson during the wedding feast, which had just begun when Samson presented his guests with a challenge. He posed a riddle. If they could give him the right answer, he would give them thirty linen tunics and thirty articles of clothing; however, if they were unable to tell him the correct answer, they must give him thirty linen tunics and thirty articles of clothing. When they agreed to the conditions, he gave them the riddle: "Out of the eater came something to eat. Out of the strong came something sweet."

The feast continued for seven days, and no one could answer the riddle. Finally, the companions went to Samson's wife and told her to coax the answer to the riddle from her husband or they would set her father's house on fire. She harassed Samson with pleading and tears. She continued to pester him and told him that if he loved her, he would tell her the answer. Finally, after all her nagging, he told her.

Afraid of her countrymen, Samson's wife told them the answer. Before sunset that day, not only the companions but also the townsmen came to Samson with the answer: "What is sweeter than honey, and what is stronger than a lion?" Samson knew immediately that his wife had told them the answer. Her disloyalty made him angry, and he considered their marriage over.

Burning with humiliation, Samson went to the Philistine city of Ashkelon, forty kilometers away, and killed thirty men. He cut down thirty innocent people on the street and stole their clothes to bring back to the companions to fulfill his agreement.

Following the collapse of his marriage, Samson returned to his parents' house. He licked his wounds and, at the time of the wheat harvest, returned to Timnah. He carried a baby goat as a peace offering and attempted to visit his wife. However, her father had already given her to one of the companions at the wedding. The father offered Samson his younger daughter instead; Samson was enraged.

Samson set out to get even. He caught three hundred foxes, tied them in pairs tail to tail, placed lit torches between each pair of tails, and turned them loose in the wheat fields of the Philistines. The townsmen retaliated for this barbaric act by taking revenge on the person who had brought this disaster upon them, the young woman. They burned her and her father to death.

After punishing the Philistines, Samson took refuge in the cave of the rock of Etam. Disillusioned with society, he lived as a virtual hermit. Unfortunately, the Philistines wanted revenge. They prepared for battle and headed for Judah. The men of Judah, frightened by the Philistine mobilization, asked why they were planning to make war on Judah. The Philistines told them that they had come to take Samson prisoner. Instead, three thousand men of Judah visited Samson at the rock of Etam and asked why he had brought war upon them. They reminded him that the Philistines ruled them.

The men of Judah told Samson that they had come to turn him over to the Philistines. His only request was that they would not injure him. They promised not to torture or kill him. They tied him up in two new ropes and led him to the Philistines at Lehi, which in Hebrew means "jaw." The Philistines greeted Samson with cheers.

Samson burst out of his ropes and picked up the raw jawbone of an ass, with which he killed a thousand Philistines. Following this massacre, Samson was weak and thirsty. He called out to God and asked if he were to die of thirst after being granted this great victory. God split open "the hollow which is at Lehi," and water gushed from it.

From Lehi, Samson went to Gaza to seek the company of a woman. It is questionable why he chose to go to Gaza where the woman would surely turn him over to her countrymen, who would put him into the hands of Philistines. Indeed, when the Gazans learned that he was in the city, they waited for him at the gates that he had to pass through to leave the city. They planned to capture him at daybreak, but he left in the middle of the night and surprised the ambushers.

Samson grasped the doors of the city gates together with the two gateposts and pulled them out along with the bar. He loaded the gates and gateposts on his shoulders and carried them to the top of the hill near Hebron.

Subsequently, Samson fell in love with a woman named Delilah in Nahal Sorek. Not much was known of Delilah, including whether she was a Philistine; however, she was the first woman in the story identified by name. The lords of the Philistines went to her and said, "Coax him and find out what makes him so strong, and how we can overpower him. Tie him up and make him helpless, and we'll each give you eleven hundred shekels of silver." Some stories portray Delilah as a tragic figure with no intention of harming Samson. These portrayals are in the minority.

Delilah asked Samson to tell her the secret of his strength. He told her, "If I were to be tied with seven fresh bow strings that were never dried, I should become as weak as an ordinary man." Delilah tied him up with the cords and cried out, "Samson, the Philistines are upon you!" Samson immediately broke the cords. Delilah was angry and accused him of lying to her.

Delilah asked Samson again how he could be tied up and restrained. He told her, "If I were to be bound with new ropes that had never been used, I would become as frail as an ordinary man." Delilah took a set of new ropes, tied him up, and said again, "Samson, the Philistines are upon you!" Samson easily snapped these ropes also. Delilah chastised him for not being truthful and again asked how he could be tied up. This time he told her, "If you weave the seven locks of my hair with the warp-threads on a loom, then I will surely weaken."

Samson fell asleep, and Delilah wove his hair on a loom with a warp-thread and also pinned it with a peg to hold it firm. She said a third time, "Samson, the Philistines are upon you!" Samson woke up and in one motion pulled out the weave and the peg. Delilah was again upset. Finally, Samson decided he should tell the woman that he loved the truth. He told Delilah, "No razor has ever touched my head, for I have been a Nazirite to God since I was in my mother's womb. If my hair were cut, my strength would leave me and I should become as weak as an ordinary man."

Delilah sensed that this time Samson was telling her the truth. She summoned the Philistine leaders and informed them that she had finally learned the secret of Samson's strength. She demanded the silver they had promised her. Delilah cut off the seven locks of Samson's hair while he was asleep on her lap. Again, Delilah cried out, "Samson, the Philistines are upon you!" He woke up thinking that he would break loose as he did the previous times. However, when he flexed his muscles, he found that "the Lord had departed from him."

The Philistines rushed into the room and gouged out Samson's eyes. They bound him with bronze chains and took him to Gaza, where he was put to work as a mill slave in the prison. He trudged endlessly turning the grindstone, stripped of his superhuman strength. He worked for many days in prison, and his hair began to grow back. One day Samson's guards took him from prison and brought him before a cheering crowd at the temple. The Philistine nobles were gathered to offer a sacrifice to their god Dagon for delivering Samson into their hands. They made him dance to humiliate him.

Samson was the only Israelite among three thousand Philistines at the temple. A small boy stood beside him to hold his hand and lead him. He asked the boy to place his hands on the pillars of the temple. Samson put one hand on the right pillar and one hand on the left pillar, "the two middle pillars that the temple rested upon."

Samson cried out, "Oh Lord God, please remember me and give me strength just this once." Samson pushed against the pillars with all of his strength. As the pillars began to crack, he realized that his God had not abandoned him after all. The temple crashed down on the Philistines and on Samson with them. It was written, "Those who were slain by him as he died outnumbered those who had been slain by him when he lived." Men of Manoah's household came to Gaza to retrieve his body; they buried him in the tomb of his father between Zorah and Eshtaol.

Moral: At times, loyalty should be questioned. Also, subduing your
      adversaries doesn't necessarily prevent them from winning
      the next round.

Based on: David Grossman, *Lion's Honey: The Myth of Samson*,
      and Mario Ruiz, *Samson: Judge of Israel*

The Golden Touch of King Midas

King Midas lived in Phrygia, now Turkey, in the eighth century BC.
He had more gold than anyone in the world; nevertheless, it was not
enough. He lusted for gold. He was most happy when he added
gold to his treasury, which was located in great vaults beneath his
palace. He spent many hours every day counting it.

King Midas was devoted to his young daughter Marygold. He
wanted to make her the richest princess in the world. Marygold had
no interest in being rich. She liked her garden and the outdoors
more than any riches that her father could provide. Marygold was
lonely; her father was so busy adding gold to his vault or counting
it that he spent little time with her. He never told her stories or went
for walks with her as most fathers did.

One day King Midas went into his treasury, locked the massive
doors, took a seat, and opened his great chests of gold. He loved to
touch it; he smiled as he let gold coins slip through his fingers and
pile up on the table. The clink of coins was music to his ears.
Suddenly a shadow fell over him and his gold. He looked up and
saw a stranger dressed in white looking down at him. King Midas
stood up suddenly. He couldn't believe that he hadn't bolted the
doors.

The stranger smiled and observed that King Midas had much
gold. The king agreed but complained about how little he had compared with all the gold in the world. The stranger asked him if he
was satisfied, and Midas admitted that he wasn't. He told the
stranger that he often stayed awake all night planning ways to
obtain more gold. King Midas wished that everything he touched
would turn to gold. The stranger asked him if he was sure of that.
King Midas said that of course he was, and that nothing would
make him happier.

The stranger told King Midas that he would be granted his wish. When the first rays of the sun came through his window the next morning, he would have the golden touch. Abruptly, the stranger disappeared. King Midas thought that he must have been dreaming. He marveled at how happy he would be if it were true.

The next morning King Midas awoke when the first faint sunlight came into his sleeping suite. He put out his hand and touched the covers of his bed. Nothing happened. He thought to himself that the stranger's promise couldn't be true. At that moment the first rays of the sun came through Midas's window, and the covers under his hand turned to pure gold. He was overjoyed that his wish had come true.

King Midas jumped out of bed and touched everything in sight. His dressing gown, his slippers, the bedroom furniture, all became gold. He looked out the window at Marygold's garden. He decided to surprise her; he ran down and touched all of her flowers, turning them into gold. He thought to himself how pleased she would be. He went back to his bedroom to wait for his breakfast. He picked up the book that he had been reading, but as soon as he touched it, it turned into gold. He couldn't read it; however, he preferred having the gold.

When the servant came with breakfast, King Midas thought how good it looked. He reached first for a ripe, red peach, but as soon as his hand touched it, it became a lump of gold. Next he picked up a roll and that too became gold, as did a glass of water. He realized that he had a serious problem. He was hungry and thirsty, but he couldn't eat gold.

At that moment, Marygold came into the room. She was crying bitterly. King Midas asked what was wrong. She held a rose in her hand. She asked her father what had happened to her garden. All of her roses had become stiff, ugly things that wouldn't grow any more. Her father told her that they were gold and asked if they weren't more beautiful than before. Marygold told him that she preferred roses that were alive and smelled good.

King Midas told Marygold to eat her breakfast. She noticed that her father looked sad and was not eating. She asked what the matter was and went over and put her arms around him and kissed him. He kissed her and suddenly cried out in anguish. When he touched her, her face became gold. She could not see, and she could not kiss him back or hold him. She was no longer a loving, happy little girl; she was a golden statue.

King Midas lowered his head and was shaken by great sobs. The stranger appeared and asked why Midas wasn't happy. The king asked how he could be happy; he was the most miserable man in the world. The stranger noted that Midas now had the golden touch and asked if that wasn't enough. The visitor asked what he would rather have, food and a cup of water or these lumps of gold. King Midas did not answer. Then the stranger asked if he would rather have a little daughter who could run, laugh, and love him or a golden statue.

King Midas told the stranger that he would give up all his gold if Marygold were brought back. He admitted that he had lost everything worth having. The stranger observed that Midas was wiser than before and told the king to plunge into the river that flowed at the foot of the garden and then to take some of its water to sprinkle on everything that he would like to change back to the way it had been.

King Midas went to the river and jumped in. He filled a pitcher with water and ran back to the palace. First, he sprinkled the water over Marygold. Color came back to her cheeks, and she opened her blue eyes and asked what had happened. King Midas cried with joy as he took her into his arms. He no longer had any interest in gold. The only gold that he cherished was the gold of the sunshine and the gold of Marygold's hair.

Moral: Be careful what you wish for; you might get it. Wealth
　　　doesn't guarantee happiness.

Based on: Nathaniel Hawthorne, "The Golden Touch,"
　　　The Wonder Book

Daniel and the Fiery Furnace

Nebuchadnezzar drove the Egyptians out of Asia and annexed Syria to the Babylonian empire. In 604 BC, he succeeded his father, Nabopolassar, on the throne of Babylon. Nebuchadnezzar was a man of unorthodox religious beliefs. He erected an golden image almost a hundred feet tall on the plain of Dura near Babylon and ordered all people in his realm to fall down and worship it. The king commanded all princes, rulers, and nobles in the land to attend a great gathering at which the image was to be dedicated for worship.

The Jewish hero, Daniel, and his friends Shadrach, Meshach, and Abednego, who had been taken captive and brought to Babylon, were also commanded to attend. The three friends attended the gathering as ordered, but Daniel was not able to be there.

The sound of trumpets and the roll of drums was the signal for all to kneel down and worship the great golden image. Everyone knelt except for the three men, who refused. The three young Jews would kneel down only for the Lord God.

Many nobles were jealous of these young men because they had been elevated to high places in the kingdom. These nobles, who hated Daniel and his friends, were glad to see that they had not obeyed the command of King Nebuchadnezzar. The king had said that anyone who did not worship the golden image would be thrown into a fiery furnace.

The scheming nobles went to the king and told him that when the music sounded for everyone to kneel down and worship the golden image, three men did not, even though they had been made rulers in the land. They were Shadrach, Meshach, and Abednego. The nobles then reminded the king he had said that all who did not worship the golden image would be thrown into a furnace of fire.

Nebuchadnezzar was filled with rage that anyone would disobey his command. He sent for the three men and told them that he would give them one more chance to kneel and worship the idol. If they did not, they would be thrown into the fire. The young men were not afraid of the king. They told him that the God they served was able to save them from the fiery furnace, and that they knew he would save them. However, even if were God's will that they should die, they would not serve the king's gods or worship the golden image.

Nebuchadnezzar gave orders to build a fire hotter than any previous fire and to throw the three Israelites into it. The king's soldiers seized them as they stood nearby in loose robes and head coverings. They tied Shadrach, Meshach, and Abednego with ropes, dragged them to the mouth of the furnace, and threw them into the fire. Flames rushed from the open door with such intensity that the soldiers who held them were burned to death. The three bound men fell down into the middle of the furnace.

King Nebuchadnezzar stood in front of the furnace and looked through the open door. He was filled with awe at what he saw. He asked the nobles standing near him if they had not seen three bound men thrown into the fire. He asked how it could be that he saw four men loose, walking in the furnace, and the fourth man looking as though he were a son of the gods. When the flames lessened, the king approached the door of the furnace and called out to the men within: "Shadrach, Meshach, and Abednego, you who serve the most high God, come out of the fire and come to me."

They came out and stood before the king, within sight of all the princes, nobles, and rulers. Everyone could see that they were alive. Their garments had not been scorched nor their hair singed. No smell of fire was upon them. King Nebuchadnezzar told his rulers: "Blessed be the God of these men, who has sent his angel and saved their lives. I make a law that no man in my kingdoms shall say a word against their God, for there is no other god who can save in this manner. And if any man speaks a word against their God, the Most High God, that man shall lose his life and his house shall be torn down." After saying this, the king promoted the three young men to even higher places in the land of Babylon.

Moral: Be steadfast in your beliefs, even when the penalty
         is severe.

Based on: Jesse Lyman Hurlbut, "The Fiery Furnace,"
         Hurlbut's Story of the Bible for Young and Old

St. George and the Dragon

Centuries ago when chivalry was still alive, one brave knight who distinguished himself was Sir George. He was so good, kind, and noble that people called him St. George. No robbers threatened people who lived near his castle; they knew that St. George would protect them. Wild animals were either killed or driven away so children could play in nearby woods without fear.

One day St. George traveled around the countryside and saw men busy at work in the fields, women singing at work in their homes, and children cheerfully at play. He noted that the people were all safe and happy. He concluded that they didn't need him anymore. He thought, "But somewhere perhaps there is trouble and fear. There may be someplace where little children cannot play in safety. A woman may have been carried away from her home, or perhaps there are even dragons left to be slain. Tomorrow I shall ride away and never stop until I find work that only a knight can do."

Early the next morning, St. George put on his shining armor and helmet and fastened his sword to his belt. Then he mounted his great white horse and rode out of his castle gate down the steep, rough road. He sat straight and tall and looked brave and strong as one would expect of a noble knight. He rode through the village and into the countryside where he saw rich fields filled with grain; peace and plenty were everywhere.

St. George rode on until he came to a part of the country that he had never seen before. No one was working in the fields, and the houses he passed were empty and silent. A wheat field had been trampled and burned, and the grass along the road had been scorched. St. George drew up his horse and look around the countryside. Desolation and silence were everywhere. He asked himself, "What can be the dreadful thing that has driven people from their homes?" He was determined to find out and to help them if he could.

Unfortunately, there was no one around to ask, so St. George rode on until he saw the walls of a city. He was sure that he would find someone who could tell him the cause of the desolation, so he spurred his horse. As he approached the city walls, the great gate opened, and he saw crowds gathered inside the walls. Some people were weeping, and all of them seemed afraid.

As St. George watched, he saw a beautiful young woman dressed in white, with a scarlet girdle around her waist, walk through the gate by herself. The gate was closed and locked after her; she walked down the road, weeping. She did not see St. George, who rode over to her. When he reached her side, he asked why she was crying. She said, "Oh, Sir Knight, ride quickly from this place. You do not know the danger you are in."

St. George said, "Danger! Do you think a knight would flee from danger? Besides, you, a fair girl, are here alone. Do you think a knight would leave you so? Tell me your trouble so that I may help you."

She cried out, "No! No! Hurry away. You would only lose your life. A terrible dragon is nearby. He may come out at any moment. One breath of fire would destroy you if he found you here. Go! Go quickly!"

St. George said, "Tell me more. Why are you here alone to meet this dragon? Are there no men left in the city?"

The maiden said, "My father, the king, is old and feeble. He has only me to help him take care of his people. This terrible dragon has driven them from their homes, carried away their cattle, and ruined their crops. They have all come within the walls for their safety. For weeks now, the dragon has come to the very gates of the city. We have been forced to give him two sheep every day for his breakfast.

"Yesterday there were no more sheep left to give. The dragon demanded that unless a young maiden were given to him today, he would break down the walls and destroy the city. The people cried to my father to save them, but he could do nothing. I am going to give myself to the dragon. Perhaps if he has me, he may spare our people."

St. George said, "Lead the way, brave princess. Show me where this monster may be found." When the princess saw St. George's flashing eyes and strong right arm as he drew his sword, she was no longer afraid. Turning, she led the way to a shining pool. She whispered, "That's where he stays. See the water move. He is waking up."

St. George saw the head of the dragon emerge from the surface of the water. He crawled out of the pool. When he saw St. George, he roared in rage and plunged toward him. Smoke and flames flew from his nostrils, and he opened his great jaws as though he were about to swallow both knight and horse.

St. George yelled, waved his sword over his head, and rode at the dragon. The blows from St. George's sword came rapidly and furiously. It was a terrible battle. Finally, the dragon was wounded. He howled with pain and plunged at St. George, opening his mouth close to the brave knight's head. St. George aimed carefully and then struck with all of his might straight down the throat of the dragon, who fell dead at his horse's feet.

St. George shouted for joy at his victory. He called the princess, who came and stood beside him. He asked her for the girdle around her waist, which he wound around the dragon's neck. He used it to pull the dragon back to the city so the people could see that it would never harm them again.

When they saw that St. George had brought the Princess back safely and had slain the dragon, people threw open the gates of the city and shouted with joy. The king came out of the palace to see why they were shouting. When he saw that his daughter was safe, he was the happiest of all. The king said, "Oh brave knight, I am old and weak. Stay here and help me guard my people from harm."

St. George agreed to stay for as long as he was needed. He lived in the palace and helped the old king take care of his people. When the old king died, St. George was made his successor. The people were happy and safe as long as they had such a brave and good man for their king.

Moral: The strong should come to the aid of the weak.

Based on: J. Berg Esenwein and Marietta Stockard,
      "St. George and the Dragon," *Children's Stories and How to Tell Them*

Chapter 2

NOTABLE / LOYAL

Our generation can produce glory and honor and undying fame.
Faith and loyalty are still able to lift common men to greatness.

Gerald White Johnson, *In Praise of England*

Androcles and the Lion

Androcles was a Roman slave who lived during the time of Tiberius. While living in Africa, he entered a cave to escape from the cruelties of his master. There he fell asleep. He was awakened by the loud roar of a lion that had entered the cave. At first Androcles was terrified that the angry lion would attack him. He soon noticed that the lion wasn't angry but in pain because its paw had been hurt.

Androcles lifted the paw to determine the nature of the injury. The lion kept still and then rubbed his head against his Androcle's shoulder. It was as though the lion were indicating that he knew the man would help him. Androcles found a long, sharp thorn in the lion's paw. He grasped the thorn and gave it a strong, quick pull. The thorn came out, making the lion so happy that he licked his new friend.

Androcles had no fear of the lion after this; in fact, they slept side by side. The lion brought food to him every day. They lived happily together in the cave for many days until Androcles was caught by Roman soldiers traveling through the woods. They recognized him and took him back to Rome. Roman law at the time dictated that a slave who ran away from his master must upon his capture fight a hungry lion in the Coliseum. A lion was selected for Androcles and locked up without food. A time was scheduled for the spectacle.

Thousands crowded into the Coliseum to see another human suffer and die. These events were the spectator sport of the time. Androcles was led into the arena. He was terrified by the roar of the lion. He looked up at the faces of the crowd and could see neither pity nor mercy, just the anticipation of being entertained. The gate was opened, and the lion reached the man in a single bound. Androcles cried out, not with fear but with happiness, because the lion was his friend from the cave.

The crowd, who expected to see the man devoured, could not figure out what was happening when Androcles put his arms around the lion. They saw the lion lie down at the man's feet and begin to lick them and then rub its head against the man's shoulder. The crowd was puzzled and called out for an explanation of what they were seeing.

Androcles placed his arm around the lion's neck and described how he and the lion had lived together in the cave and become friends. The crowd, who had been looking forward to being entertained, realized that they had observed something extraordinary. They were no longer bloodthirsty but called out repeatedly for the slave to be freed. The crowd's wishes were granted, and Androcles was given his freedom. The lion was released to him, and they lived together happily for many years.

Moral: Help those in need. Hopefully, good deeds will be reciprocated.

Based on: James Baldwin, "Androcles and the Lion,"
Favorite Tales of Long Ago

Daniel in the Lions' Den

The lands that earlier had been the Babylonian and Chaldean empires became the empire of King Darius of Persia. When Daniel was a very old man, Darius installed him in a high place of honor and power. Daniel was first among the rulers of the empire because he was wise, and Darius knew that he ruled well. Other princes and rulers were jealous of Daniel. They tried to find something evil in Daniel, so they could speak against him to the king.

These jealous men knew that three times every day Daniel went to his room, opened the window facing Jerusalem, and prayed to God. At the time, Jerusalem was in ruins, and the temple had been destroyed. Nevertheless, Daniel prayed every day, facing toward the site where the temple had stood, even though it was hundreds of miles away.

The princes and rulers who wished to speak out against Daniel thought that in Daniel's prayers, they could find an opportunity to cause him harm. They approached King Darius with a proposal agreed upon by all the rulers. They suggested enacting a law that for thirty days no one should ask anything from any god or man, except for the king. Anyone who prayed to god or asked anything from another man during the thirty days would be thrown into the lions' den. Then they asked the king to sign the law, which could not be changed. No law of the Medes or the Persians could be altered.

King Darius was foolish and vain. This law pleased him because it set him above the gods. He signed the law without asking his nobles' advice. The announcement was sent through the kingdom that for thirty days, no one should pray to any god or ask a favor of any man.

Daniel was aware of the law, but, as before, he went to his room, faced toward Jerusalem, and prayed to the Lord three times a day. The jealous princes and rulers watched him closely and confirmed that he was still praying to God as he had done earlier. They went to King Darius and asked if he had made the law that anyone in thirty days who offered a prayer would be thrown into the den of lions. The king agreed that the law had been enacted, and that it must stand.

They told the king that one man did not obey his law, and that it was Daniel, one of the captive Jews. They reported that Daniel prayed to God three times a day, just as he had done before the law was signed. The king regretted what he had done. He loved Daniel and knew that no one in the kingdom was as trustworthy. All day long, King Darius tried without success to think of a way to save Daniel's life. That evening, the men returned and reminded the king that the law he had made must be kept.

Reluctantly, King Darius sent for Daniel and ordered him to be thrown into the den of lions. He told Daniel he hoped that his God, to whom he was so faithful, would save him. Daniel was led to the pit where the lions were kept and thrown in. Over the mouth of the pit was placed a heavy stone, which the king sealed with his personal seal and the seals of his noblemen to prevent anyone from letting Daniel out of the den.

King Darius returned to his palace. He could not eat. He did not listen to the music that usually relaxed him. He could not sleep; he thought only of Daniel. He awoke early and went to the lions' den. He broke the seals, had the stone removed, and sorrowfully called out to Daniel. He didn't expect to hear him, only the roar of lions. He asked Daniel if his God had been able to save him from the lions.

King Darius heard the voice of Daniel coming from the den, saying, "Oh king, may you live forever! My God has sent his angel and has shut the mouth of the lions. They have not hurt me, because my God saw that I had done no wrong. And I have done no wrong to you, oh king!" The king was relieved and ordered his servants to help Daniel out of the den. He was brought out without harm because he trusted in the Lord.

The king commanded that the princes and rulers who had spoken against Daniel be thrown into the lions' den. As soon as they fell to the floor of the den, they were set upon by the lions and torn into pieces.

King Darius wrote to all of the people in all his empires, "My peace be given to you all abundantly! I make a law that everywhere among my kingdoms men fear and worship the Lord God of Daniel, for he is the only living God, above all other gods, who could save him."

Moral: Respect your fellow man even though he may have
different beliefs. With unwavering faith, much can be
accomplished.

Based on: Jesse Lyman Hurlbut, "Daniel in the Lions' Den,"
Hurlbut's Story of the Bible for Young and Old

The Three Questions

It once occurred to a king that if he always knew the right time to begin everything, if he knew who were the right people to listen to and whom to avoid, and, above all, if he always knew the right thing to do, he would never fail in any undertaking. He proclaimed throughout his kingdom that he would give a sizable reward to anyone who could teach him what the right time for every action was, who the necessary people were, and how he might know the most important thing to do.

Learned men responded to the king, but they all answered his questions differently. Some said that in order to know the right time for every action, one must draw up, in advance, a table of days, months, and years and then live strictly according to it. Only then, they reasoned, could everything be done at its proper time. Others claimed that it was impossible to decide beforehand the right time for every action; but that, not letting oneself become absorbed in idle pastimes, one should attend to all that was going on and then do what was most needed.

29

Still others said that however attentive the king might be to what was going on, it was impossible for one man to decide correctly the right time for every action; he should have a council of wise men, who would help him find the proper time for everything. Others said that some things could not wait to be placed before a council, but it must be decided at once whether to undertake them. Unfortunately, in order to decide, one must know beforehand what was going to happen. Only astrologers know that; therefore, in order for the king to know the right time for every action, astrologers must be consulted.

Conflicting answers were given to the second question as well. Some said that the people the king needed the most were his counselors, others said priests, still others said doctors, and a few said that warriors were the most necessary.

For the answer to the third question, the most important occupation, the king was advised by some that the most important thing in the world was science. Others considered it skill in warfare, while still others said that it was religious worship. Since all the answers were different, the king disagreed with all of them and gave the reward to no one. He decided to consult a hermit who was widely known for his wisdom.

The hermit lived in the woods and never ventured out into society. He received only common people, so the king put on peasant clothes and dismounted from his horse before reaching the hermit's hut. He left his bodyguard behind. When the king approached, the hermit was digging in the ground in front of his hut. He greeted the king and continued to dig. The hermit was old and frail. He breathed heavily each time he stuck the spade into the ground and overturned the earth.

The king walked up to him and said, "I have come to you, wise hermit, to ask you three questions: How can I learn to do the right thing at the right time? Who are the people I need most, and, therefore, to whom should I pay more attention than the rest? Also, what activities are the most important and need my attention first?

The hermit stopped digging, listened to the king, and then resumed digging. He did not answer. The king noticed that the hermit was tired and offered to take the spade and dig for awhile. The hermit gave the spade to the king, thanked him, and sat down on the ground. After the king had dug two vegetable beds, he stopped and repeated his questions.

Again, the hermit did not answer. He reached for the spade and suggested that the king rest for awhile. Nevertheless, the king continued to dig until an hour passed and then another. When the sun began to sink behind the trees, the king stuck the spade upright in the ground and said, "I came to you, wise man, for answers to my questions. If you have no answers for me, tell me so, and I will return home."

The hermit observed that someone was running toward them. He suggested that they find out who it was. The king turned and saw a bearded man running out of the woods. The man held his hands pressed against his stomach, and blood was flowing from under them. When he reached the king, he fell fainting on the ground and moaned feebly. The king and the hermit unfastened the man's clothing, revealing a large wound in his stomach. The king washed the wound and bandaged it with his handkerchief and with a towel provided by the hermit.

The blood would not stop flowing, and the king repeatedly removed the bandage and washed and rebandaged the wound. Finally, the blood stopped flowing, and the man revived and asked for a drink of water. The king brought fresh water and gave it to him. Meanwhile, the sun had set, and it had become cool. The king, with the help of the hermit, carried the man into the hut and laid him on the bed. The man closed his eyes and was quiet.

The king was so tired from the work he had done that he crouched down and was soon asleep. When he awoke the next morning, it took him awhile to remember where he was and who the stranger lying on the bed was. When the bearded man saw that the king was awake and looking at him, he asked his forgiveness in a weak voice. The king responded that he did not know him; therefore, there was nothing to forgive.

The man said to the king, "You do not know me, but I know you." He told the king that he was an enemy who had sworn to take revenge on him for executing his brother and seizing his property. The man knew that the king had gone alone to see the hermit and had resolved to kill him on his way home. The man had waited in hiding, but the day had passed and his target did not return.

Finally, the man had come out of his ambush to look for the king and stumbled upon the bodyguard, who recognized and wounded him. He had escaped but would have bled to death if the object of his revenge had not dressed his wound. His life had been saved by the man he had come to kill. Again, he asked the king's forgiveness. He offered to serve the king loyally from then on and to convince his sons to do the same.

The king was happy to have made peace with his enemy and to have gained him as a loyal friend. He not only forgave him but also offered to send servants and a physician to attend to him. Furthermore, the king promised to restore the family property to him. The king left the bearded man to rest and went looking for the hermit. The hermit was outside, on his knees, sowing seeds in the beds that had been dug the day before. The king approached the hermit and asked one more time for answers to his three questions. The hermit looked up and told the king that his questions had already been answered. The king asked what he meant.

The hermit answered that if the king had not pitied the hermit's weakness and dug the vegetable beds, the king would have headed home in time to be attacked by the man. The hermit pointed out that the most important time for the king was when he was digging the beds, and that the most important man was the hermit. The king's most important business was to do the hermit a good turn.

The hermit added that afterwards, when the man ran to them, the most important time was when the king was attending to the man and that if the king had not bound up the wound, the man would have died without making peace. Therefore, the wounded man was the most important man, and what the king did for him was the most important business.

The hermit advised the king: "There is only one time that is important—Now! It is the important time because it is the only time when we have any power. The most necessary man is the one with whom you are, for no one knows whether he will ever have dealings with anyone else. The most important lesson is to do good to others, because for that purpose alone is man sent into this life!"

* * *

Never let success hide its emptiness from you,
achievement its nothingness, toil its desolation.
Keep alive the incentive to push on further, that
pain in the soul that pushes us beyond ourselves.

Don't look back. And don't dream about the future,
either. It will neither give you back the past,
nor satisfy your other daydreams. Your duty,
your reward—your destiny—are here and now.

Dag Hammarskjold, *Markings*

Moral: The present is the most important time, because it is the
only time we can control. The past is history, and the future,
at best, is only a plan.

Based on : Leo Tolstoy, "Three Questions," *Walk in the Light
and Twenty-Three Tales*

Icarus and Daedalus

Daedalus was the most skillful craftsman and inventor in ancient
Greece. He built magnificent palaces with extensive gardens and
created many works of art, including statues so beautiful that they
looked real. Greeks had such a high regard for the works of
Daedalus that they thought he must have learned his craft from the
gods. His reputation was known far beyond Greece.

King Minos of Crete needed a way to control a terrible monster
called the Minotaur that was half man and half beast. Minos had
heard about the cleverness of Daedalus and invited him to Crete to
build a prison for the Minotaur. Daedalus and his son, Icarus, sailed
to Crete and built the famous Labyrinth, a maze of winding passages and turnings opening into one another in a manner so tangled
that whoever went in could never find a way out. The Minotaur was
confined to the maze.

When the Labyrinth was finished, Daedalus wanted to return
with his son to Greece, but Minos kept them in Crete to invent more
wonderful things for him. He locked Daedalus and Icarus in a high
tower overlooking the Mediterranean Sea. Minos knew that
Daedalus was clever enough to escape from retention, so he had
every ship that left Crete searched for stowaways before departure.

From his high tower, Daedalus watched the seagulls soaring on
the breezes from the Mediterranean. He thought, "Minos may control the land and sea, but not the air. We will go that way." He gath-

33

ered a large pile of feathers of all sizes, sewed them together with thread, and molded them with wax. He made two great wings that curved like those of a bird. With the help of Icarus, he fitted himself with wings fastened to his shoulders. After a few unsuccessful efforts, he found that by waving his wings he could rise into the air. Daedalus held himself aloft and maneuvered in the air currents until he could soar like a bird.

Next Daedalus built a second set of wings for Icarus and fitted them to his son's shoulders. He taught Icarus how to ride the air currents; they practiced until the boy was ready. Daedalus said, "Icarus, I charge you to keep at a moderate height, for if you fly too low sea sprays will clog your wings; if you fly too high, the heat of the sun will melt the wax, and your wings will fall apart. Stay close to me and you will be safe."

Then Daedalus flew out of the tower, and Icarus followed him. As the ground of Crete passed beneath father and son, plowmen stopped their work to gaze at them, and shepherds stared skyward, wondering if they were seeing gods in flight. At first flying seemed terrifying. After the two passed Samos and Delos on the left and Lebynthos on the right, they gained confidence. They lost their fear and began to enjoy the experience.

Icarus sensed a freedom he had never known before and began to fly higher and higher. He could see the blue sea beneath him and the sails of many ships. He soared higher and higher, forgetting his father's warning. Daedalus called out to him repeatedly, but Icarus either could not hear him or did not heed him. Icarus was enthralled with his new environment.

Eventually, as Icarus got closer to the sun, the wax holding his wings together began to melt. One by one the feathers fell off and scattered. Then the wax all melted at once, and Icarus could no longer stay airborne. He cried out to his father, but it was too late. He fell from his lofty height and plunged into the sea, disappearing beneath the waves.

Daedalus circled over the water repeatedly, but he saw nothing but feathers floating on the surface. He knew that his son was gone. At last the body came to the surface, and Daedalus recovered it from the sea. He buried Icarus in a land he called Icaria in memory of his son. Daedalus hung up his wings and, with a broken heart, never flew again.

Moral: Elders should be obeyed, particularly parents.

Based on: Milton Rugoff, "Daedalus, Icarus, and the Wings,"
   A Harvest of World Folk Tales

The Legend of the Minotaur

This legend begins in Athens, one of the greatest cities in ancient Greece. At the time, however, Athens was a small town perched on top of a cliff. King Aegeus, who ruled Athens in those days, had just welcomed home his son, Theseus, whom he had not seen since birth.

Aegeus was happy to have his son home at last, but Theseus noticed that his father seemed distracted and sad. He also perceived a melancholy among the people of Athens. Mothers were quiet, fathers shook their heads, and children watched the sea all day, as if they expected something fearful to come from it. Many Athenian youths were missing and were said to be visiting relatives in other parts of Greece.

At last Theseus asked his father what troubled the land. Aegeus told his son that he had returned at an unhappy time. A curse so terrible had been placed upon Athens that not even he, Prince Theseus, could deal with it. The trouble dated back to a time when young men came to Athens from all over Greece and other countries to participate in the Panathenaic Festival, which involved contests in distance running, boxing, wrestling, and foot races. Androgeus, the son of King Minos of Crete, was among the victors. He was killed by Athenians, who were jealous of the victories he had won. His comrades left immediately to bear the news to Crete.

The sea was soon black with King Minos's ships seeking vengeance. Minos's army was too powerful for Athens. Athenians went out and begged him for mercy. He said that he would not burn the city or take the people captive. However, he told Athenians that they must pay him a tribute. Every nine years, they must choose by lot seven young men and seven maidens and send them to him. Athens had no choice but to agree. Every nine years a ship with black sails arrived from Crete and took away the captives. This was the ninth year, and the ship was due soon.

Theseus asked what happened to the young people when they reached Crete. Aegeus admitted that they didn't know because none of them had ever returned. However, the sailors of Minos said that the captives were placed in a strange prison, a kind of maze called the Labyrinth. It was full of dark twisting passageways and occupied by a horrible monster called the Minotaur. This creature had the body of a man, the head of a bull, and the teeth of a lion; he devoured everyone that he encountered. Aegeus said he feared that had been the fate of the Athenian youths.

Theseus suggested that they burn the black-sailed ship when it arrived and slay the sailors. Aegeus objected because that would cause Minos to return with his navy and army and destroy Athens. Theseus then asked to be allowed to go as one of the captives, so he could slay the Minotaur. He claimed it as his right as Aegeus's son and heir. Theseus considered it his duty to free Athens from this awful curse.

Aegeus tried to discourage his son from this plan. However, Theseus was determined and when the ship with the black sails entered the harbor, he joined the doomed group. His father wept when he came to see Theseus off. He asked Theseus that if he did come back alive to lower the black sails as he approached and raise white sails. Aegeus would then know that his son had survived the Labyrinth. Theseus told Aegeus not to worry but to look for white sails, since he would return in triumph.

The ship put to sea and reached Crete after sailing for many days. The Athenian prisoners were marched into the palace, where King Minos sat on his throne, surrounded by courtiers clothed in silken robes and ornaments of gold. Minos fixed his eyes on Theseus. Theseus bowed and met the king's gaze. Minos observed that the captives were fifteen in number, but that his tribute claimed only fourteen.

Theseus told him that he had come of his own will. Minos asked him why, and he said that the people of Athens wanted to be free. Minos agreed that if Theseus slew the Minotaur, Athens would be absolved of the tribute. Theseus said that he planned to slay the Minotaur, causing a stir in the court. A beautiful young woman glided among them and stood just behind the throne. This was Ariadne, Minos's daughter, a wise and tender-hearted maiden. Theseus bowed low and then stood erect with his eyes on the face of Ariadne.

Minos told Theseus that he spoke like a king's son, perhaps

someone who had never known hardship. Theseus replied that he had known hardship and that his name was Theseus, Aegeus's son. He asked the king to let him face the Minotaur alone. If he could not slay it, his companions would follow him into the Labyrinth. Minos responded that if Aegeus's son wanted to die alone, he could do so.

The Athenian youths were led upstairs and along galleries, each to a chamber more rich and beautiful than they had seen before, even in their dreams. Each was taken to a bath, washed and clothed in new garments, and then treated to a lavish feast. None of them had sufficient appetite to eat, except Theseus who knew he would need his strength.

That evening, as Theseus was preparing for bed, he heard a soft knock on his door. Suddenly, Ariadne, the king's daughter, was standing in his room. Once again Theseus gazed into her eyes and saw there a kind of strength and compassion that he had never encountered before. She told Theseus that too many of his countrymen had disappeared in the Labyrinth, and that she had brought him a dagger and could show him and his friends the way to escape. He thanked her for the dagger but said that he couldn't flee. He was going to take on the Minotaur.

Ariadne warned Theseus that even if he could slay the Minotaur, he would have to find his way out of the Labyrinth. She told him that it had many dark twists and turns and so many dead ends and false passages that not even her father knew its secrets. She took from her gown a spool of thread and pressed it into his hand. She said that if he were determined to go forward with his plan he should tie the end to a stone as soon as he entered the Labyrinth and unwind the thread as he wandered through the maze. The thread would guide him out.

Theseus looked at her, not knowing what to say. He asked why she was doing this, knowing that she would be in trouble if her father found out. She told him that if she didn't, he and his friends would be in greater danger. Theseus knew then that he loved her.

The next morning Theseus was led to the Labyrinth. As soon as the guards had shut him inside, he tied one end of the thread to a rock. He began to walk slowly, keeping a firm grip on the precious string. He went down the widest corridor, from which others turned off to the left and to the right, until he came to a wall. He retraced his steps, tried another hallway, and then another, always listening for the monster.

Theseus passed through many dark winding passageways, gradually descending further and further into the Labyrinth. Finally he reached a room that was piled high with bones, and he knew he was near the beast. Theseus sat still and from far away heard a sound, like the echo of a roar. He stood up and listened intently. The sound, like that of a bull but thinner, came nearer and nearer. Theseus scooped up a handful of dirt from the floor and drew his dagger with the other hand.

The roars of the Minotaur came nearer and nearer. Theseus could hear the thudding of feet along the floor. He squeezed into a corner of the passageway and crouched there. His heart was pounding. Catching sight of him, the Minotaur roared and rushed straight at him. Theseus leaped up and, dodging aside, threw the handful of dirt into the monster's eyes. The Minotaur, shrieking and confused, rubbed his eyes. Theseus crept up behind the beast and slashed at his legs. The Minotaur fell with a crash, biting at the floor with his lion's teeth.

Theseus waited for his chance and then plunged the dagger into the Minotaur's heart three times. He kneeled and thanked all the gods. When he finished his prayer, he hacked off the head of the Minotaur. Clutching the monster's head, he followed the thread out of the Labyrinth. It seemed that he would never find his way out of those dark, gloomy passageways. It took so long he wondered if the string had snapped somewhere, and he had lost his way. Finally he came to the entrance and fell to the ground, worn out from his struggle.

Minos was surprised when he saw the Minotaur's head in the grip of Theseus. The king kept his word, however, and gave Theseus and his friends the freedom he had promised. Minos wished for peace between Crete and Athens and bade Theseus and his friends farewell.

Theseus knew that he owed his life and his country's freedom to Ariadne's courage. He felt that he could not leave Crete without her. One version of the legend is that Theseus asked Minos for his daughter's hand in marriage, and that the king consented. Another version has Ariadne stealing aboard the departing ship at the last moment without her father's knowledge. Either way, the two lovers were together when the anchor lifted and the dark ship sailed from Crete.

Unfortunately, this happy ending is mixed with tragedy, as legends sometimes are. The Cretan captain of the vessel did not know that he was supposed to hoist white sails if Theseus came home in triumph. King Aegeus, as he anxiously watched from a high cliff, saw the black sails coming over the horizon. The thought of losing his son broke his heart. He fell from the towering cliff into the sea, which is now called the Aegean Sea.

Moral: Courage is required to right a wrong. Compassion can guide courage.

Based on: Andrew Lang, "The Minotaur,"
The Book of Romance

Chapter 3

SELF-DETERMINED / RESPONSIBLE

Responsibility: A detachable burden easily shifted
to the shoulders of God, Fate, Fortune, Luck,
or one's neighbor. In the days of astrology
it was customary to unload it upon a star.

Ambrose Bierce, *The Devil's Dictionary*

The Tale of Sulayman Bey

A young Arab had just married and had given the customary feast for his new wife's relatives and friends. When the festivities were over, the groom accompanied his guests to the door, but he neglected to shut it before returning to his wife. When they were alone, his wife turned to him and asked him to go and close the street door.

The young bridegroom asked why he should do it. As a new groom clothed in silk, wearing a shawl, and with a dagger set in diamonds, he did not see why he should be the one to close it. The young wife asked why she as a new bride, robed in a satin dress with lace and precious stones, should have to go and close the door, particularly since he was the one who had left it open. She asked her husband to make a bargain that the first one to speak should go and close the door.

The husband agreed. They sat down and looked at each other in silence for several hours. During this time, thieves passed by and, seeing the door open, came in and took everything they could carry away. The young couple heard the footsteps but didn't speak. The robbers even came into the room in which the couple were seated, motionless and indifferent to all that took place.

The robbers continued their pillage, collecting everything valuable, including the carpets under the couple. Then the thieves removed anything of value from them, while they remained silent in fear of losing the wager. The robbers left quietly after having cleared out the house. The young married couple remained silently in their chairs.

The next morning a police officer came around on his tour of inspection and, seeing the door open, walked in. He searched all the rooms leading to the room in which the bride and groom were seated. He walked into the room where they were and asked the meaning of what he saw. Neither of the young people replied.

The policeman grew angry and threatened to stick his dagger into the young groom to make him talk. Just before he did, the young wife cried out that the man was her husband and asked that he be spared. The groom laughed, clapped his hands, and exclaimed that he had won the bet; therefore, she should go and close the door. They explained the bargain to the policeman, who shrugged and left. The young couple was left in a barren house, facing the expense of replacing the stolen property.

Moral: Pride and stubbornness should not take precedence
        over reason.

Based on: W. A. Clouston, "Sulayman Bey and the Three
           Storytellers," *Popular Tales and Fictions*

The Maiden and the Morning Star

One night a beautiful Iroquois maiden slept outside the door of her
lodge on sleeping robes spread in the tall grass. While she slept, a
shaft of light from above fell upon her face and seemed to touch her
gently. When she awoke, she realized that the light had come from
the Morning Star up above in Sky Land.

The caress of the tender glow moved her so deeply that she fell
in love with the source of the silvery radiance from the heavens.
She pledged that she would never marry a mere mortal; she would
wed the Morning Star or no one. She stared upward toward Sky
Land every night until the brightness of the sun caused the light of
the morning star to fade. She watched her celestial lover at night
and thought about him all day.

One morning she went to a spring near her lodge and was surprised to see a handsome brave whom she did not know. He smiled
and told her that he was the Morning Star. He said that he knew she
had been looking at him, and that he also knew what was in her
heart. He asked her to marry him, and she accepted his proposal.
Morning Star removed a long, yellow plume from his hair and
handed it to her. As soon as she grasped it in her hand, she was lifted into Sky Land, where she was welcomed into Morning Star's
lodge.

She lived in her husband's lodge in comfort and was free to go
anywhere she chose. Her only restriction was that she was not to go
near a strange golden plant that grew outside their lodge. One day
she could not contain her curiosity any longer, and she pulled the
plant out of the ground to see what was beneath it. She found that
the hole through which she had entered Sky Land was underneath
the curious plant. When she looked through the hole, she could see
the people of her village on earth below. She heard the voices of her
friends. She became very homesick and began to cry.

Morning Star found his wife weeping and knew immediately

what she had done. He commanded her to return to her people. She returned to earth on silvery strands like a strong spider web. Her exile from Sky Land saddened her, and every evening she walked up a nearby hill, lifted her arms skyward, and begged to be reunited with her husband.

One evening Morning Star replied to her prayers. He told her that she could never be forgiven; she would never be allowed to return to Sky Land. She was heartbroken to hear this, and the next day she could not be found. Villagers searched the top of the hill, but she had disappeared. They found a tree growing in the place where she had lifted her arms skyward in prayer. They were not familiar with the strange tree whose branches seemed to droop downward in sadness. The tree is now known as the weeping willow.

Moral: Curiosity must be controlled to be considered a virtue.
Unfortunately, some decisions are irrevocable.

Emerson Klees, "The Maid Who Fell in Love with the
Morning Star," *More Legends and Stories*

The Diamond Necklace

Mathilde Loisel was one of those attractive, charming ladies, born, as if through an error of destiny, into a family of clerks. She had no dowry, no hopes, no means of becoming known, loved, or married by a man either wealthy or distinguished. She married a petty clerk who worked for the Board of Education.

Mathilde dressed simply, not being able to adorn herself. She was unhappy, as one out of her class, although she had qualities that make some daughters of the people the equal of great ladies. She suffered from the poverty of their apartment: the shabby walls, the worn chairs, and the faded pillows. The sight of her humble husband awoke in her sad regrets and desperate dreams of intimate drawing-room conversations with men friends, whose attention all women desired.

When Mathilde dined at home with her husband, who truly liked and complimented her on her pot pie, she thought of elegant dinners, shining silver, and exquisite food served on marvelous dishes, accompanied by whispered gallantries. She had neither frocks nor jewels, nothing. And she loved those things and thought that she was made for them. She had a rich friend, Mrs. Forestier, a schoolmate at the convent, whom she envied but did not like to visit because she suffered so much upon her return home.

One evening her husband came home with a smile on his face and a large envelope in his hand. He told her that the envelope was for her. She opened it and drew out a printed card with the words, "The Minister of Public Instruction and Madame George Pamponneau ask the honor of Mr. and Mrs. Loisel's company Monday evening, January 18, at the Minister's residence." Instead of being delighted, she threw the invitation spitefully on the table and asked her husband what she was supposed to do with it.

Her husband replied that he thought she would be happy with an opportunity to go out. He told her that the invitation was very select, and that not many were given to employees. She would see the whole official world there. She asked him what she was supposed to wear to a function like that. He suggested the dress that she wore to the theater. He could see that she was upset and asked what was wrong. She said that because she had nothing to wear, he might as well give the invitation to a colleague whose wife was better fitted out than she.

Her husband asked how much it would cost to buy a suitable gown, something simple that would serve for other occasions. She said that four hundred francs would be needed. He turned a little pale, for he had saved just that sum to buy a gun to join some friends in hunting parties next summer on the plains at Nanterre. The loving husband told her that he would give her four hundred francs for the dress.

The day of the ball approached and Mathilde seemed disturbed and anxious. Fortunately, her dress was nearly ready. Her husband asked her why she had been acting strangely. She said she was sad because she did not have a jewel, not one stone, nothing with which to adorn herself. She thought that she would have the appearance of poverty, and that she would rather not go. He suggested wearing natural flowers. She said there was nothing worse than looking shabby in the company of genteel women.

Loisel suggested that she contact her friend Mrs. Forestier and ask to borrow her jewels. She knew Mrs. Forestier well enough to ask this favor. Mathilde visited her friend the next day and described her dilemma. Mrs. Forestier took out a large jewelry box, brought it to her friend, and told her to chose anything she wanted. Mathilde saw a black satin box containing a beautiful diamond necklace. She asked her friend if she could borrow the necklace, only the necklace. She embraced her friend in thanks.

Mathilde was a great success at the ball. She was elegant, gracious, and the prettiest woman there. All the men asked to be presented to her, and all the cabinet members waltzed with her. The Minister of Education paid considerable attention to her. She danced with enthusiasm, intoxicated by the admiration she received. The Loisels did not leave for home until four o'clock in the morning.

Loisel motioned for a cab in the street, but they were unable to get one. They walked toward the Seine River and finally found a cab near the docks. When they arrived home, Mathilde removed her wrap and looked in the mirror. She uttered a cry. The diamond necklace was not around her neck. They looked everywhere and could not find it. Her husband asked if she had it on when they left the minister's house. She said that she had. They thought that if it had fallen in the street, they would have heard it drop.

They realized that they must have lost it in the cab, but they didn't remember the cab's number. Loisel retraced their steps but found nothing. He visited the police and the cab offices and placed an advertisement in the newspapers, offering a reward. No sign of the necklace appeared. Loisel suggested to his wife that to give them a little time she write Mrs. Forestier and tell her that the clasp had broken, and that she was having it fixed.

By the end of the week, they had lost all hope. Mathilde had aged five years. They realized they were responsible for replacing the necklace. They took the black satin box to the jeweler whose name was inscribed inside. He told them that he had only furnished the box, not the necklace. They went from jeweler to jeweler, looking for an identical necklace. Finally in a shop on the Palais-Royal, they found a diamond necklace exactly like the one they had lost. It was valued at forty thousand francs, but they could have it for thirty-six thousand.

The Loisels asked the jeweler to hold it for three days and made arrangements to return it for thirty-four thousand francs if they found the other necklace before the end of the month. Loisel had eighteen thousand francs his father had left him, and he borrowed the rest. He gave notes, made ruinous promises, borrowed from usurers, and compromised his whole existence. He didn't know whether he could ever repay his loans. He was anxious about the future. When Mathilde returned the jewels to Mrs. Forestier, her friend told her that they should have been returned earlier, because they might have been needed. Mrs. Forestier did not detect the substitution, however.

Many changes were necessary in the Loisel household. The couple sent away their maid and changed their lodgings to rented rooms. Mathilde washed the dishes, did the laundry, and hauled the refuse to the street. Clothed like a woman of the people, she haggled with shopkeepers over every sou. Every month some notes had to be renewed to gain time. Loisel worked evenings and did odd jobs.

By the end of ten years, they had paid all their debts with interest. Mathilde seemed old now. She had become a hard, crude woman who dressed badly and spoke loudly. Sometimes when she took a break from her household duties, she reminisced about that evening party ten years ago and of their changed circumstances now. How would it have been if she had not lost the necklace? Who knows? Life is full of changes, and how small a thing can ruin or save us!

One Sunday, as she was walking along the Champs-Elysees to forget the cares of the week, Mathilde encountered a woman walking with a child. It was Mrs. Forestier, still young and still pretty. Mathilde was affected by the chance meeting and wondered whether she should speak to her and tell her about the necklace, now that she had paid. Why not?

Mathilde approached her old friend and said, "Good morning, Jeanne." Her friend did not recognize her and was surprised to be addressed by a common woman. Mathilde identified herself to Mrs. Forestier.

Mrs. Forestier uttered a cry of astonishment and commented on how much her friend had changed. Mathilde admitted to experiencing hard times since they had last met, and that it was all because of her. Mrs. Forestier asked how the hard times could be her fault. Mathilde asked her friend if she remembered lending her the necklace for the Minister's Ball. Mrs. Forestier remembered. Mathilde then admitted to losing it, even though Mrs. Forestier believed it had been returned. Mathilde confessed that she had replaced it with an identical necklace, and that it had taken ten years to pay for it. Since they were without means, she admitted that it had been very difficult.

Mrs. Forestier stopped short and asked if she understood correctly that her friend had bought a diamond necklace just like hers. Mathilde confirmed that she had. She smiled with a proud and simple joy. Mrs. Forestier, however, was moved and took both her friends hands in hers. "Oh! My poor Mathilde! Mine were false. They were not worth over five hundred francs!"

Moral: Stepping up to responsibility is noble. However, verifying facts can prevent unfortunate results due to false assumptions.

Based on: Guy de Maupassant, "The Diamond Necklace," *The Best Stories of Guy de Maupassant*

The Legend of the Peace Queen

A Iroquois maiden known for her good judgment was chosen to act as arbitrator of disputes among nations of the Iroquois Confederacy. The sachems provided her with a lodge deep in the forest and called her Genetaska, the Peace Queen. Iroquois women considered her a sacred being. Her word was law and could not be contested.

One afternoon while hunting in the woods, an Oneida brave killed a buck with an arrow through the heart. After he had skinned the deer and was about to cut it into quarters, an Onondaga brave stepped out from the trees and said that the kill belonged to him. He claimed that he had fatally wounded the buck before the Oneida brave shot his arrow to finish him off. Their argument became heated, and they came to blows and fought for several hours, with neither gaining advantage over the other.

Finally, the exhausted braves decided to present their disagreement to the Peace Queen for resolution. She scolded them for fighting within her domain, directed them to divide the deer equally, and told them to return to their villages. However, the Onondaga brave was smitten by the beauty of the Peace Queen and did not want to return home. He proposed to her and asked her to share his lodge. She told him that she could not marry because of her sacred duty to the Iroquois Confederacy. The Onondaga brave prepared to return to his village.

The Oneida brave also had fallen in love with the Peace Queen. She refused his offer of marriage as well, but she responded so softly and affectionately that he could not get her out of his mind. She asked the two braves to leave in peace. They were reconciled and became friends with the common bond of unrequited love for the same woman.

However, Genetaska thought about the Oneida brave all the time—upon waking, during the day, and while falling asleep in the evening. Many moons passed while the Peace Queen fulfilled her obligation to the Iroquois to settle disputes. However, her heart was heavy with longing for the brave, gentle Oneida warrior.

One day she was pining for him as she warmed herself by the fire, and he appeared before her. He looked pale and haggard and explained that he could not live without her. He had lost interest in the hunt, and he no longer enjoyed playing lacrosse and other games with his friends. He admitted that the light had gone out of his life, and he asked again for her hand in marriage. This time, she agreed to become his wife. She regretted walking away from her sacred obligations, but she thought that she would wither away if she did not marry the one she loved. She and her brave traveled to their new home.

The chiefs who had elected her Peace Queen to settle disputes were angry with her for abandoning her responsibilities. They tore down her lodge in the woods and abolished the position of Peace Queen. As might be expected, arguments and fights resumed within the Iroquois Confederacy.

Moral: Live up to your responsibilities. The Peace Queen was selfish to place personal interests before the good of the Iroquois Confederacy.

Emerson Klees, "The Legend of the Peace Queen,"
More Legends and Stories

The Legend of the Three Beautiful Princesses

During the time of the Moors in Spain, there reigned in Granada a Moorish king named Mohamed, whose subjects added El Hayzati, or "The Left-handed" to his name. Some say it was because he was more expert with his sinister than his dexter hand; others, because he tended to spoil everything he meddled in. He was continually in trouble.

Mohamed was driven from his throne three times, barely escaping with his life on one occasion. He was as brave as he was blundering. He wielded his scimitar wisely and each time re-established himself on the throne by hard fighting. Unfortunately, instead of gaining wisdom from adversity, he became more obstinate.

One day Mohamed and his courtiers were riding near the foot of the Elvira mountains when he encountered a band of Moorish horsemen returning from a raid into Christian Spain. They had a long string of mules laden with captives of both sexes and other spoils. Mohamed was struck by the appearance of a beautiful young woman, richly attired, who sat weeping on a palfrey. Her duenna, who rode beside her, was attempting to console her.

Mohamed was told that she was the daughter of the alcayde of a frontier fortress that had been raided and sacked. Mohamed claimed her as his royal share of the booty and conveyed her to his residence in the Alhambra. After doing everything he could to cheer her up, he asked her to be his queen. Initially, she resisted his advances. After all, he was an infidel, an enemy of her country, and he was old.

Mohamed enlisted the support of the duenna, who had been captured with the young lady. This Andalusian woman saw the advantage of his proposal and immediately argued his cause with her mistress. The duenna asked her mistress if it wasn't better to be mistress of this beautiful palace, with all its gardens and fountains, than shut up in her father's old frontier tower. The duenna told her mistress that she would be marrying the man, not his religion, and that because he was older, she would be a widow sooner and subsequently her own mistress. Finally, the young lady was reminded that she was in the king's power, and it would be better to be his queen than his slave.

The Spanish lady dried her tears, married Mohamed, and conformed, in outward appearances, to her husband's faith. The duenna became a zealous convert to Moslem doctrines and was given the Arabian name of Kadiga. After a year of marriage, the Moorish king became the proud father of triplets, three lovely daughters. He summoned his astrologers for their advice on the multiple birth. He was told that his daughters were a precarious property and would need his watchfulness when they reached marriageable age. Furthermore, he should gather them under his wings at that time and trust them to no other guardian.

Mohamed's queen bore him no more children and died within a few years of their birth. He decided to have his daughters reared by Kadiga in the royal castle of Salobrena, a sumptuous palace in a Moorish fortress on a hill overlooking the Mediterranean Sea. The palace had all kinds of luxuries. The princesses passed their lives in indolence. They were cut off from the world and attended by female slaves who anticipated their every wish. They had beautiful gardens filled with rare fruit and flowers. On three sides, the castle looked down upon a rich valley bounded by the lofty Alpuxarra mountains; the fourth side overlooked the sea.

The princesses displayed diverse temperaments. Zayda, the oldest, took the lead in everything and was inquisitive, never satisfied until she got to the bottom of things. Zorayda, the middle daughter, had a great feeling for beauty, including her own image in a mirror, and was fond of flowers, jewels, and other ornaments. Zorahayda, the youngest, was gentle, timid, and very sensitive. She looked after pet birds and animals with tenderness. She spent hours on the balcony, gazing at stars on a summer night or at the sea lit up by the moon. Over the years, Kadiga attended to her charges with faithful care.

One of the walls of the castle of Salobrena extended down the hill until it reached a jutting rock overhanging the sea, with a narrow sandy beach at its foot. A small watchtower on this rock contained a pavilion, with latticed windows to admit the sea breeze. The princesses passed the sultry hours of midday in this pavilion.

One day the curious Zayda was seated by a window and saw a galley anchoring at the base of the tower. Moorish soldiers landed on the beach with Christian prisoners. The three sisters peeked through the lattice that screened them from sight. Among the prisoners were three richly dressed Spanish cavaliers in the prime of youth. The princesses gazed with breathless interest. The only men they had seen were slaves and humble fishermen. The gallant cavaliers carried themselves with a noble presence that caused flutters in the sisters' bosoms.

Zayda asked if a nobler being had ever tread the earth than the cavalier in crimson. She was impressed with his bearing. Zorayda was attracted to the one in green and was captivated by his grace and elegance. The gentle Zorahayda said nothing, but secretly chose the cavalier in blue. The princesses watched the cavaliers until they were out of sight. They sighed and looked pensively at one another.

Kadiga found them in this condition. They described what they had seen. The duenna's heart was warmed. She told the princesses that the young men would be missed by the young ladies in their native cities. She related to the sisters the colorful tournaments and the courting and serenading of Spanish ladies. Zayda's curiosity was fully aroused; her inquiries were lengthy. The beautiful Zorayda regarded herself in the mirror when she heard of the charms of the Spanish ladies. Gentle Zorahayda sighed at the mention of moonlight serenades.

Zayda asked about the cavaliers every day, and, finally, Kadiga realized the mischief that she had caused. She had been thinking of the princesses as children; however, they had matured into attractive young women of marriageable age. It was time, the duenna thought, to talk with the king about his daughters.

One morning the king was sitting in a cool hall in the Alhambra, when a slave arrived from the fortress of Salobrena bearing a message from Kadiga congratulating him on the anniversary of his daughters' birthday. The slave also presented the king with a basket decorated with fig leaves containing a peach, an apricot, and a nectarine with their bloom and downy sweetness upon them, all in an early stage of tempting ripeness. The message was clear to the king.

The king realized the time had come that the astrologers had warned him about; his daughters were now at a marriageable age. They were shut up, away from the eyes of men and under the care of the loyal Kadiga. However, they were not under his own eye, as advised by the astrologers. He ordered that a tower of the Alhambra be prepared for them, and he left for the fortress at Salobrena to conduct them home personally.

When Mohamed greeted his daughters at Salobrena, he had not seen them for three years. He was astounded at how they had changed. They had passed across that wondrous boundary in female life that separates the unformed, thoughtless girl from the blooming, meditative woman.

The tall, well-formed Zayda entered her father's apartment with a stately step and made a profound reverence to him, treating him more like a sovereign than her father. The beauty Zorayda, of medium height, approached her father with a smile and kissed his hand. The shy Zorahayda, smaller than her sisters, had a personality of the tender, beseeching kind that sought fondness and protection. As she drew near her father with a timid step, she looked up and saw him beaming with a paternal smile. She threw herself upon his neck.

The king accompanied his daughters back to Granada, escorted by a troop of black horsemen. The princesses rode on beautiful white palfreys with gold bits and stirrups and silken bridles adorned with precious stones.

As the cavalcade approached Granada, it overtook a small company of Moorish soldiers with a convoy of prisoners. It was too late for the soldiers to get out of the way so they threw themselves face down on the ground and ordered the prisoners to do the same. Among the prisoners were the three cavaliers the princesses had seen from their pavilion. They either did not understand the order or were too proud to obey it. They remained standing and gazed at the cavalcade as it approached.

The king's ire was ignited at this flagrant defiance. He drew his scimitar and would have struck the cavaliers if the princesses had not crowded around him, imploring mercy for the prisoners. The captain threw himself at the king's feet, begging him not to cause a scandal he would regret. The captain advised that these were three brave and noble Spanish knights, who had been taken in battle after fighting like lions. He pointed out that the men were of high birth and would bring sizable ransoms.

The king agreed to spare them. He commanded that they be taken to the vermilion towers and assigned to hard labor. During the commotion, while the king was making one of his usual left-handed blunders, the veils of the princesses had been thrown back and the radiance of their beauty revealed. The hearts of the cavaliers were completely captured; gratitude was added to their admiration. The princesses were struck more than ever by the noble demeanor of the captives, enhanced by the news of their valor and lineage.

The residence provided for the princesses was in a tower connected to the main palace of the Alhambra. On one side it overlooked a garden filled with the rarest flowers. The tower was divided into beautifully decorated small apartments. In the center of the apartments was an alabaster fountain with suspended cages for songbirds, surrounded by aromatic shrubs and flowers.

The princesses should have been happy there, but they were not. Although they had been happy at the castle of Salobrena, here they were melancholy and dissatisfied with everything around them. The king didn't know what to make of this, so he contracted all the dressmakers and jewelers to provide his daughters with silk robes, cashmere shawls, and jewelry with pearls and diamonds. All this was of no avail, the princesses continued to be pale and languid. The king thought that they looked like three blighted rosebuds.

The king asked Kadiga about the secret malady preying upon his daughters. The duenna knew more about their malady than they knew themselves, but she asked them why they were so downcast when they had everything their hearts desired. The princesses looked around and sighed. Kadiga asked if they would like to be sung to by the famous singer Casem from Morocco. The young women replied that they had lost their interest in music.

Kadiga told them that they wouldn't say that if they had heard the music she had heard the previous evening from the three cavaliers they had met on the road. The duenna asked why they were blushing. They asked her to continue her story. She said that as she passed the vermilion towers, she saw the three cavaliers resting after their day's labor. One was playing gracefully on the guitar, and the other two took turns singing. They performed in such style that the guards stood motionless listening to them.

Kadiga admitted to being moved to tears by hearing the songs of her native province and by seeing three such handsome youths in captivity. The princesses asked their duenna to let them see and hear the cavaliers. They thought that music would be reviving. Kadiga reminded them of what their father would think. Young women are not necessarily put off by prohibitions, however. They begged, coaxed, and entreated that a refusal would break their hearts.

The jailer of the Christian captives confined in the vermillion towers was Hussein Baba, a broad-shouldered renegado, who was known to have an itchy palm. Kadiga visited Hussein and told him that the princesses shut up in the tower had heard of the musical talents of the Spanish cavaliers. She slipped a gold coin into his hand and asked him to let the young men play their music and sing during work breaks. The princesses would be able to hear them from the tower windows.

The next morning the cavaliers were put to work in the ravine beneath the tower. During the noontime heat, when their fellow laborers dozed and the guard nodded off drowsily, the young men sat among the greenery at the base of the tower and sang a Spanish roundelay accompanied by the guitar. The ravine was deep and the tower was high, but their voices were heard distinctly in the stillness of the early summer afternoon.

The princesses listened from the balcony. They had been taught the Spanish language by Kadiga and were moved by the tenderness of the songs. Their duenna was concerned, however, because the cavaliers were singing love songs addressed to the princesses. She threatened to go to Hussein and have the singing stopped. The young women begged her not to. Kadiga gave in because she could see that the singing had a beneficial effect on her charges. A rosy bloom had come into their cheeks, and their eyes sparkled.

When the singing ended, the princesses remained silent. Then Zorayda played the lute and with her sweet, soft voice sang an Arabian song whose message was that a rose is concealed in her leaves but listens with delight to the song of the nightingale.

The cavaliers worked almost daily in the ravine and continued their serenades. Hussein Baba became more and more indulgent and slept more frequently at his post. The princesses showed themselves at the balcony and communicated with the young serenaders by means of flowers and a symbolic language all the young people understood. The difficulties of conversing over a distance added to its charms and strengthened their passions. The change improved the appearance and lifted the spirits of the young women. No one was happier than Kadiga, who was proud of her involvement with this change.

Eventually, the cavaliers no longer appeared in the ravine. When Kadiga asked where they had been taken, she was told that the Spanish cavaliers had been ransomed by their families and were in Granada making arrangements to return home. Kadiga told the princesses that this was the way of life. Soon the young men would be back serenading their lovers under the balconies of Cordova and Seville. She told the princesses that the young men would not be thinking of the Alhambra, and that they should put the cavaliers out of their minds.

On the third day after the cavaliers had left the Alhambra, Kadiga entered the princesses' apartments ruffled with indignation. She ranted and raved about the insolence of the cavaliers, and how she had brought this on herself by conniving this deception of the king. Kadiga fumed that the cavaliers had proposed that she, the most loyal of duennas, participate in treason. The young men had dared to ask her to persuade the princesses to fly with them to Cordova and become their wives.

The old woman cried with grief and indignation. The princesses turned pale, trembled, looked down, and cast shy looks at one another, but said nothing. At last, Zayda, the leader and most spirited, went over to Kadiga, put her hand on the duenna's shoulder and asked, if they were willing, whether such a thing would be possible. Kadiga said possible, indeed; the young men had already bribed Hussein Baba to arrange the whole plan. Kadiga talked fearfully about the consequences of deceiving the king, who had placed so much confidence in her. She began to cry again.

On the other hand, Kadiga admitted, the king had treated his daughters tyrannically, keeping them shut up in the tower wasting their bloom like roses left to wither. Zayda agreed that the king had never placed any confidence in his daughters but had treated them like captives. The princesses reminded Kadiga that they would have youthful husbands in exchange for a severe old father.

Kadiga asked if they were afraid to leave the Granada of the Moors and move to a Spanish province. The sisters reminded her that they would be returning to the land and the faith of their mother. Kadiga expressed concern about being left behind to bear the brunt of their father's vengeance. The princesses asked her to accompany them.

The princesses immediately agreed on the plan, although the youngest hesitated. Zorahayda's gentle soul struggled between youthful passion and loyalty to her father, but finally, with stifled sighs, she gave in. The sisters prepared themselves for flight.

Over the centuries, the rugged hill on which the Alhambra was built had been perforated with subterranean passages leading to various parts of the city and to the banks of the Darro and Xenil rivers. They had been used by Moorish kings as a means of escape during sudden insurrections. Hussein knew of a passage that led outside the walls of the city to a place where the cavaliers would be waiting with fast horses to convey the party over the border.

When the appointed night for their escape arrived, Kadiga looked down from the balcony at Hussein, who signalled her to fasten the end of a rope ladder to the balcony railing and lower it into the garden below. The duenna climbed down first, followed by the two older princesses with thumping hearts. When it came to Zorahayda's turn, the youngest princess trembled and hesitated. Several times, she put her foot on the ladder and then pulled it back. She looked back into her apartments, where she had been secure. She wondered what dangers she would encounter out in the world.

Zorahayda's sisters implored, the duenna scolded, and Hussein swore all in vain. Every moment increased the danger of discovery. Suddenly, they heard the distant tramp of a patrol. They told Zorahayda that if she didn't come now, they would have to leave without her. Still torn about the decision, Zorahayda loosened the ladder of ropes and threw it from the balcony. The two older sisters were sad to leave their sister behind, but the advancing patrol left them no choice but to hurry to the tunnel.

They groped their way along a rough passageway to an iron gate that opened outside the walls. The Spanish cavaliers were waiting to receive them, disguised as Moorish soldiers of the guard. Zorahayda's lover was crushed when he learned that she had refused to leave the tower. The two princesses mounted behind their lovers and Kadiga rode behind the renegado. They galloped toward the Pass of Lope that led through the mountains towards Cordova.

They had not gone far when they heard the sound of drums and trumpets from the battlements of the Alhambra. They knew that their escape had been discovered. When the party reached the foothills of the Elvira Mountains, they looked back and could not see anyone following them. However, when they reached the Bridge of Pinos, they saw that the tower of the bridge blazed with light and bristled with armed men. Hussein led them off the road, skirted the river for a distance, and then plunged into its waters. They were borne downstream by the rapid current but made it safely to the other side.

They reached Cordova safely, where the cavaliers' restoration to family and friends was celebrated. The beautiful princesses were received into the Church, and the young couples began their happy lives.

Little is known of the reaction of the king when he learned that two of his daughters with the help of Kadiga and Hussein had deceived him. He guarded his remaining daughter carefully, even though she showed no interest in eloping. It was thought, however, that she secretly regretted staying behind. Frequently she could be seen leaning on the battlements of the tower, looking mournfully toward the mountains in the direction of Cordova. Sometimes the sad notes of her lute could be heard, lamenting the loss of her sisters and her lover.

Zorahayda died young. According to legend, she was buried in a vault beneath the tower, near the place where the Spanish cavaliers serenaded her and her sisters.

Moral: He or she who hesitates is lost. Many of our mistakes are errors of omission, not commission; that is, we don't do something and later regret our failure to act.

Based on: Washington Irving, "Legend of the Three Beautiful Princesses," *The Alhambra*

Chapter 4

PERSEVERING / RESOURCEFUL

It's the steady, constant driving
To the goal for which you're striving
Not the speed with which you travel,
That will make your victory sure.
It's the everlasting gaining,
Without whimper or complaining
At the burdens you are bearing
Or the woes you must endure.
It's the holding to a purpose
And never giving in;
It's the cutting down the distance
By the little that you win;
It's the iron will to do it;
So whatever your task, go to it!

Anonymous

Tamerlane and the Ant

Tamerlane, the renowned Asian conqueror from Samarkand was born in 1336. Like Alexander the Great, he was a world conqueror. His early battles were in eastern Turkestan; then he fought the Persians and the Afghans. He invaded Russia and occupied Moscow for a year. Late in his career, like Alexander, he invaded India. Tamerlane died in 1405, before he could carry out his planned invasion of China.

Tamerlane rarely suffered defeat, but after one of his few, his army scattered. He left the field of battle alone and wandered from place to place. His enemies were searching for him. He was in despair and about to lose all hope. After twenty days, he knew that he could not hold out much longer.

Tamerlane was resting at the base of a tree, thinking about his misfortunes. He saw a small object creeping up the trunk of the tree. He looked closely and saw that it was an ant carrying a grain of wheat as big as itself. Tamerlane noticed a hole in the tree just above the ant, which must have been its home. Just as Tamerlane was thinking about the heavy load that the ant had to carry, it fell to the ground. Nevertheless, it did not lose its grip on the grain of wheat.

Tamerlane watched the ant try a second time to carry his load up the rough bark of the tree. He watched the brave little insect try three times, four times, a dozen times, twenty times—always with the same result. Finally, on the twenty-first attempt, the ant made it over the rough spot where it had slipped and fallen so often. It ran into its home, carrying his precious load.

Tamerlane had wandered for twenty days; the ant had tried to get to his home twenty times. He realized that the ant had taught him a lesson. He decided to try try again, and he reassembled his army. This time they succeeded in defeating the enemy.

This tale is reminiscent of the story of Robert Bruce and the spider. The spider tried six times to reach a new location without success. It was successful on the seventh try, as was King Robert I of Scotland in winning a victory on the battlefield after six defeats.

Moral: Persevere and you will reach your goals.

Based on: James Baldwin, "Try, Try Again," *Fifty Famous People*

From Each According to His Ability

Vuyning left his club, cursing it softly. From ten in the morning until eleven his fellow members had bored him considerably. Kirk with his fish story, Brooks with his Puerto Rican cigars, old Morrison with his anecdote about the widow, Hepburn with his consistent luck at billiards—all the usual prattle had been repeated ad nauseam. In addition to these afflictions, Miss Allison had refused him again the night before. Five times she had laughed at his offer to make her Mrs. Vuyning.

Vuyning walked along Forty-fourth Street to Broadway and turned south. He wore a light gray suit, expensive kid shoes, a finely woven straw hat, and a shirt that was a light shade of heliotrope. He was dressed with a lordly carelessness, combined with an accurate conception of current fashion.

Even the customary noises of Broadway that morning provided a discord to Vuyning's ears. He was daydreaming until a lady, passing, jabbed the ferrule of a parasol in his side, bringing him back to earth. Five more minutes along Broadway brought him to a certain corner where a number of silent, pale men stood around for hours. Wall Street speculators, driving home in their carriages, liked to point out these men to their visiting friends and tell them of this well-known lounging place of the "crooks."

Vuyning was delighted when one of this company stepped forth and addressed him as he was passing. Vuyning was eager for something out of the ordinary, and to be accosted by this smooth-faced, keen-eyed member of the underworld had the taste of adventure that he was seeking.

The man said, "Excuse me, friend. Could I have a few minutes' talk with you—on the level?"

"Certainly," said Vuyning with a smile. "But let's go to a quieter place. There is a cafe across the street that will do. Schrumm will give us a quiet corner table."

Schrumm gave them a secluded table under a palm tree. Vuyning opened the conversation by talking about the weather. His companion said, "In the first place, I want you to understand that I am a crook. Out West I am known as Rowdy the Dude. Pickpocket, second-story man, burglar, cardsharp, and slickest con man west of the Twenty-third Street ferry landing—that's my history. That's to show that I'm being square with you. My name's Emerson."

"Confound old Kirk with his fish stories," thought Vuyning to himself with silent glee as he searched his pockets for a card. "It's pronounced 'Vining,'" he said as he handed it to his companion. "And I'll be frank with you. I'm just a loafer, living on my father's money. At the club, they call me 'Left-at-the-Post.' I have never done a day's work in my life. It's a pretty shabby record."

"There's one thing you can do," said Emerson admiringly, "You know how to wear clothes. You are the best-dressed man I have seen on Broadway. I'll bet that I have spent more on clothes than you have. Take a look at me. What's wrong?"

The clubman said, "Some Broadway window dresser has misused you. I can see that it is an expensive suit; however, it is six months old in cut, and your hat is last year's style. Your tan shoes would be fine for a vacation at the lake, and you should be wearing plain socks, not ones with a embroidered pattern."

Emerson said, "Give me more of it. Say, you're the right kind of swell. Anything else odd about the way I dress?"

Vuyning said, "Your tie is tied with precision and correctness."

"Thanks, I spent a half-hour tying it before I—"

Vuyning interrupted, "Thereby completing your resemblance to a dummy in a Broadway store window."

Emerson said, "Thanks for putting me wise. I knew that there was something wrong, but I just couldn't put my finger on it."

Vuyning, whose ennui had taken wings, offered to take his companion to his tailor. Expense was not an issue, for Emerson admitted to robbing a bank recently in the Midwest. Vuyning asked Emerson if he wasn't afraid that he would turn him over to the police.

Emerson said coolly, "You tell me why I didn't keep them." He laid Vuyning's pocketbook and watch—the Vuyning 100-year-old family watch—on the table. As they left to visit the tailor, Vuyning thought how much more interesting this was than his club.

Five days later at the club, Vuyning told his friends that he would be bringing a friend of his from the West to dine at their table that evening. They asked if he was current on the Denver financial scene and knowledgeable of fishing west of the Mississippi River. Vuyning told his friends that his guest had none of those vices; he was a burglar and a safecracker and a friend of his. They asked why Vuyning had to adorn every statement with a weak attempt at

61

humor.

At eight o'clock that evening, a smooth, affable man sat at Vuyning's right hand at dinner. When the conversation moved to the Czar in Russia or to fishing in Rocky Mountain streams, this faultlessly dressed visitor disposed of all subjects with ease. Then he painted for them with broad strokes a majestic panorama of the West. He spoke of snow-topped mountains and pine-filled gorges, sweeping the clubhouse into rapt attention. He opened a new world to their view.

The visitor talked about cowboys with lariats and Colt "forty-five" revolvers as well as the ravages of "redeye" whiskey in border towns. He spread the broad range of the West before them, describing vast square miles of sagebrush and mesquite. He told of camps and ranches marooned in a sea of fragrant prairie blossoms and of gallops on horseback in the still of the night. He painted for them the great, rough epic of cattle drives through unspoiled hills and plains.

Vuyning met Emerson the next morning at ten o'clock at a cafe on Forty-second Street. Emerson was leaving for the West later that day. He wore a suit of dark cheviot that appeared to be ahead of the styles. He thanked Vuyning for his advice on dressing well and offered to return the favor at any time. Vuyning asked, "What was that cowpuncher's name who caught a mustang by the nose and mane and threw him until he put the bridle on?"

"Bates," said Emerson.

"Thanks," said Vuyning. "I thought it was Yates." Vuyning also remembered another piece of Emerson's advice: "Bacon, toasted on a greenwillow switch over red coals, ought to put broiled lobsters out of business."

"And you say that a horse at the end of a thirty-foot rope can't pull a ten-inch stake out of wet prairie? Well, goodbye, old man, if you must be off. Good luck."

At one o'clock Vuyning had luncheon with Miss Allison. For thirty minutes he babbled to her about ranches, horses, canyons, windstorms, roundups, the Rocky Mountains, and beans and bacon. She look at him with wondering eyes. Vuyning concluded, "I was going to propose again today, but I won't. I've worried you often enough. You know my father has a ranch in Colorado. What's the good of staying here? It's great out there. I'm leaving for Colorado next Tuesday."

"No, you won't, not alone" said Miss Allison, dropping a tear in her salad.

Vuyning asked what she meant.

"What do you think?"

"Betty!" exclaimed Vuyning, "What do you mean?"

Miss Allison said that she would go, too. Vuyning filled her glass with wine. He gave a mysterious toast to Rowdy the Dude. Miss Allison said, "I don't know him, but if he's your friend, Jimmy—here goes."

Moral: If the straightforward approach fails repeatedly,
        try going around the barn.

Based on: O. Henry, "From Each According to His Ability,"
        The Voice of the City

The Old Man and the Gold Crowns

One day years ago, Vanillo Gonzales, a page for the Duke of Ossuna, governor of Sicily, was approached on the street by a young citizen of Palermo. The young man feared that his old father would be ruined unless the governor's influence could be obtained in his behalf. The young man convinced Gonzales to go home with him and hear the tale from his father's own lips.

The old man told Gonzales how, six months earlier, Charles Azarini, Peter Scannati, and Jerom Avellino had come came to his house accompanied by a notary public. They brought with them ten thousand crowns in gold and informed him that they had agreed to deposit the money with him until they found a good investment opportunity.

They gave him the money to safeguard and requested an agreement in writing that he would not deliver it, or any part of it, to one of them except in the presence of the other two. He entered into this agreement by signing a document prepared by the notary public. They deposited the money with him until delivery to the three parties was requested.

A few nights later, Jerom Avellino knocked on the father's door in great agitation, asked for pardon for the interruption, and told him that the importance of the business at hand required it. Avellino said that he, Azarini, and Scannati had learned that a richly laden ship from Genoa had just arrived at Messina, providing them with an excellent investment opportunity if they acted quickly. They had decided to invest the ten thousand crowns deposited with the old man. Avellino asked for the deposited funds to be immediately given to him. His horse was waiting at the door for a fast ride to Messina.

When the old man reminded Avellino that the money could not be given to him without the other two men present, Avellino interrupted and told him that Azarini and Scannati were ill and couldn't come to the house but had agreed to allow Avellino to act for them and to absolve him from the agreement. Avellino said that they must act immediately or lose the opportunity to invest.

Avellino pointed out that he had known the old man for a long time and had always been regarded as a man of good character. He hoped that any unjust suspicion on the old man's part would not now disturb the friendship that had existed between them. The father hesitated for a long time, concerned about breaking the agreement. However, Avellino coaxed and tormented the old man, until at last his resistance failed. Foolishly, he gave the deposit to Avellino, who left in a hurry.

At the end of his narrative, the old man cried at his foolishness. Vanillo Gonzales consoled him assuring him that the governor was powerful and that it would be difficult for Avellino to escape justice. The old man's son told Gonzales that Avellino was far away and out of reach, and that the main concern was the suit brought by Azarini and Scannati against his father to restore the ten thousand crowns to them. The suit was to be heard within two days. The page said that he would notify the governor of the circumstances, and that the governor would probably try the suit personally.

Two days later, the viceroy summoned the parties to appear before him. After the plaintiffs had presented their case, the governor asked the defendant what response he had to the plaintiffs' request. The old man admitted that he had none. The governor noted that since the old man had no defense, he must pay the plaintiffs the ten thousand crowns that had been deposited with him. However, the viceroy reminded the plaintiffs that the defendant could not, by the terms of the agreement, deliver the funds unless all three parties were present.

Azarini and Scannati were ordered to bring Avellino into court, and they would receive the money. As soon as this ruling was announced, the crowded courtroom was filled with applause. The verdict was discussed on street corners in every city in Sicily.

Moral: Justice usually prevails. Sometimes that justice is creative.

Adapted from: W. A. Clouston, "The Three Glaziers and
the Alewife," *Popular Tales and Fictions*

A Message to Garcia

Early in the Spanish-American War in 1898, it was necessary for the U.S. Government to communicate quickly with General Garcia, the leader of the insurgents in Cuba. Unfortunately, no one knew where in the mountain fastnesses of Cuba he was. No mail or tele-graph message could reach him. President McKinley needed to secure his cooperation, and quickly.

Someone told the President that a fellow by the name of Rowan could find Garcia, if anyone could. Rowan was sent for and given a letter to be delivered to the insurgent general. Rowan took the let-ter, sealed it in a oilskin pouch, and strapped it over his heart. In four days he landed by night off the coast of Cuba in a open boat and disappeared into the jungle. Three weeks later, he came out on the other side of the island, having traversed a hostile country on foot and delivered his letter to Garcia.

McKinley gave Rowan a letter to be delivered to Garcia. Rowan took the letter without asking, "Where is Garcia?" Here is a man whose form should be cast in bronze and the statue placed in every college in the land. It is not book learning young men need, nor instruction about this or that, but a stiffening of the vertebrae that will cause them to be loyal to a trust, to act promptly, and to concentrate their energies and just do it—"Carry a message to Garcia."

General Garcia is dead now, but there are other Garcias. Every man who has endeavored to carry out an enterprise where many hands are needed has been appalled at times at the imbecility of the average man—the inability or unwillingness to concentrate on one thing and do it. Slipshod assistance, foolish inattention, casual indifference, and half-hearted work seem the rule; and no man succeeds unless, by hook or by crook, or threat, he forces or bribes other men to assist him; or maybe, God in his goodness performs a miracle and sends him an Angel of Light for an assistant.

Put this matter to a test. Suppose you are sitting in an office; six clerks are within call. Summon one and make this request: "Please look in the encyclopedia and make a brief memorandum for me concerning the life of Correggio." Will the clerk quietly say, "Yes, sir," and go and do the task? He will not. He will look at you askance and ask one or more of the following questions:

Who was he?

Which encyclopedia?

Where is the encyclopedia?

Was I hired for that?

Don't you mean Bismark?

What's the matter with Charlie doing it?

Is he dead?

Is there any hurry?

Shall I bring you the book and let you look it up yourself?

What do you want to know for?

Ten to one says that after you have answered the questions, and explained how to find the information, and why you want it, the clerk will get one of the other clerks to help him try to find Correggio—and then come back and tell you there is no such man. Of course, I may lose the bet. If you are wise, you will not bother to explain that Correggio is under the C's, not the K's, but will go and look it up yourself.

This incapacity for independent action, this moral stupidity, this infirmity of will, this unwillingness to catch hold and lift— these are things that put socialism so far into the future. If men will not act for themselves, what will they do when the benefits of their efforts are for all? Advertise for a stenographer, and nine out of ten who apply can neither spell or punctuate—and do not think it is necessary to. Can such a one write a letter to Garcia?

A foreman in a large factory pointed out the bookkeeper and observed that he was a fine accountant, but if he was sent out on an errand he might accomplish it or he might not. He might stop at four saloons along the way and by the time he reached Main Street would forget what he had been sent for. Can such a man be entrusted to carry a message to Garcia?

Much is said about unfair treatment of workers. Little is said about the employer who grows old before his time in a vain attempt to get employees to do intelligent work and not loaf when his back is turned. In every store and factory, a constant weeding-out process is going on. It is survival of the fittest. Self-interest motivates every employer to keep the best—those who can carry the message to Garcia.

Some brilliant men do not have the ability to manage a business of their own and yet are absolutely worthless to anyone else, because they are constantly suspicious that their employer is oppressing or intending to oppress them. They cannot give orders, and they will not receive them. If a message were given to them to take to Garcia, they would probably say, "Take it yourself."

In fairness, let us drop a tear too for the men who are striving to carry on a great enterprise and whose working hours are not limited by the whistle, whose hair is fast turning white through the struggle to hold in line careless indifference, slipshod imbecility, and heartless ingratitude.

Has the matter been put too strongly? Possibly. A word of sympathy is deserved for the man who succeeds—the man who against great odds has directed the efforts of others and, having succeeded, finds there is not much in it. Respect is deserved for the man who does his work when the boss is away as well as when the boss is at home. And the highest respect is due the man who, when given a message to Garcia, quietly takes the missive without asking any idiotic questions and with no intention of chucking it or doing other than delivering it.

Civilization is one long, anxious search for just such individuals. Anything such a man asks shall be granted. His kind is rare; no employer can afford to let him go. He is wanted in every city, town, and village—in every office, shop, store, and factory. The world cries out for such workers; they are needed and needed badly—those who can carry "A message to Garcia."

Moral: Sometimes a point can best be made by overstatement.
Be responsible; just do it.

Based on: Elbert Hubbard, "A Message to Garcia,"
A Message to Garcia and Other Essays

Mammon and the Archer

Old Anthony Rockwall, retired manufacturer and proprietor of Rockwall's Soap, looked out the library window of his Fifth Avenue mansion and grinned. His neighbor to the right—the aristocratic clubman, G. Van Schuylight Suffolk-Jones—came out to his waiting motor car, wrinkling a nostril at the front of his nouveau riche neighbor's soap palace. Anthony laughed at his stuck-up, old-wealth neighbor and went to the door to call his servant, whom he asked to summon his son.

When young Rockwall entered the library, the old man set aside his newspaper and gave his son a kindly look. Richard, only six months home from college, did not know what to make of his sire. Anthony told his son that he was a gentleman, and that they say that it takes three generations to make one. The father observed that they were wrong, money can make a gentleman in one generation. It had made his son one and almost had made one of him. Anthony commented that he himself was nearly as impolite as the two old knickerbocker gents on each side of him who couldn't sleep nights because he had bought the house between their homes.

Richard replied that money couldn't buy everything. His father disagreed and asked what money could not buy. His son replied that it couldn't buy into the exclusive circles of society. His father asked where the exclusive circles of society would be if the first Astor hadn't had the money to pay for his steerage passage over.

Richard sighed. His father asked him what was wrong. Anthony had noticed a change in his son over the previous two weeks. He told his son that if he needed a vacation, the *Rambler* was down in the bay, fueled, and ready to steam to the Bahamas in two days.

Richard told his father that it was a good guess, and that he hadn't missed by much. Anthony asked, "What is her name?" Richard began to walk up and down the library floor. His father might be crude, but he had enough comradeship and sympathy to draw Richard out.

Anthony demanded, "Why don't you ask her to marry you? She'll jump at you. You've got the money and the looks, and you're a decent fellow. Your hands are clean; you've got no Eureka soap on them. You've been to college, but she'll overlook that."

Richard admitted that he hadn't had a chance to talk with her alone. Anthony suggested that he make his own chance: walk her home from church or take her for a walk in the park. Richard told his father that she was caught up in the social mill. Every minute and every hour of her time was arranged for days in advance. He admitted to his father that he must have this girl, or this town would be a dismal swamp. The old man asked his son why, with all the money they had, he could not get an hour or two of the girl's time for himself.

Richard admitted that he had hesitated too long, and that she was going to sail the day after tomorrow to Europe for a visit of two years. He told his father that she was staying with an aunt in Larchmont, and that he could see her alone the next evening for only a few minutes. Her schedule permitted him to pick her up in a cab at Grand Central Station, meeting the 8:30 train. Then they would drive down Broadway to the theater, where her mother and friends would meet her in the lobby.

Richard asked his father if he thought she would listen to a proposal from him in six or eight minutes under those circumstances. He would have no opportunity in the theater or after the show. Richard added that this was one dilemma that money could not solve. Time cannot be purchased with cash. If it could, rich people would live longer. There was no hope of getting a chance to talk with Miss Lantry before she sailed. Anthony told his son to run along to his club, commenting that he was glad to hear that the young man wasn't in need of a vacation.

That evening Richard's Aunt Ellen came into the library while her brother Anthony was reading his evening paper and talked about the lovers' woes. Anthony told his sister that Richard had mentioned his amatory problem, but that when offered the use of his father's bank account, he declared that money couldn't help. The rules of society couldn't be changed by a team of millionaires.

Aunt Ellen chastised her brother and told him that she wished he wouldn't think about money so much. She said, "Wealth is nothing where true affection is concerned. Love is all-powerful. If he had only spoken earlier! She could not have refused our Richard. But now I fear it is too late. He will have no opportunity to talk with her. All your gold cannot bring happiness to your son."

The following evening at eight o'clock Aunt Ellen took an old gold ring from a beat-up case and gave it to Richard. She urged, "Wear it tonight, nephew. Your mother gave it to me. She said it brought good luck in love. She asked me to give it to you when you found the one you loved." Young Rockwall took the ring reverently. He tried it on his little finger but it wouldn't fit, so he stuffed it into his vest pocket. Then he telephoned for a cab.

Richard led Miss Lantry out of the mob at Grand Central Station at eight thirty-two. She cautioned Richard not to keep her mother and the others waiting. Richard directed the cab driver to take them to the theater as fast as he could. They sped down Forty-second Street to Broadway and turned left on Broadway toward the theater. At Thirty-fourth Street, Richard asked the cab driver to stop. He mumbled something about dropping a ring that had been his mother's, which he didn't want to lose. He said that he saw it fall, and he would recover it quickly. He was back in the cab in less than a minute.

Within that minute a crosstown streetcar stopped directly in front of the cab. The cabbie tried to pass to the left, but a heavy express wagon cut him off. He tried going to the right but was blocked by a furniture van that had no business being there. When he tried to back up, he swore because he couldn't. He was blockaded in a tangled mess of vehicles. Miss Lantry expressed concern about being late.

Richard looked around and saw a congested flood of wagons, trucks, cabs, vans, and streetcars filling the vast space where Broadway, Sixth Avenue, and Thirty-fourth Street cross one another. Vehicles were still hurrying from the cross streets toward the converging point at full speed, hurling themselves into the straggling mass. The oldest spectator among the crowds lining the sidewalks had never witnessed a street blockade of the proportions of this one.

Richard apologized to Miss Lantry and said that it was probably his fault. If he had not dropped the ring, it might not have happened. She asked to see the ring and added that she thought that theaters were stupid anyway.

At eleven o'clock that night someone tapped lightly on Anthony Rockwell's door. Anthony, who was in his dressing gown reading a book about pirate adventures, called out, "Come in."

Aunt Ellen entered. "They're engaged, Anthony. She has promised to marry our Richard. On their way to the theater there was a street blockade, and it was two hours before their cab could get out of it. And oh, brother Anthony, don't ever boast of the power of money again. A little emblem of love—a ring that symbolized unending and unmercenary affection—was the cause of our Richard finding his happiness. He dropped it in the street and got out to recover it. Before they could continue, the blockade occurred. He spoke to his love and won her there while the cab was hemmed in. Money is worthless compared with true love, Anthony."

"All right," said old Anthony. "I'm glad the boy has got what he wanted. I told him I would spare no expense in the matter if—"

"But, brother Anthony, what good could your money have done?" she chided.

The next day a man with puffy red hands and a blue polka-dot tie, who called himself Kelly, called at Anthony Rockwall's house and was received in the library. "Well," said Anthony, reaching for his checkbook, "It worked. Let's see, you had $5,000 in cash."

"I paid out $300 more of my own," said Kelly. "I had to go a little above the estimate. I got the express wagons and cabs, mostly for $5; but the trucks and two-horse teams mostly raised me to $10. The motormen wanted $10, and some of the loaded teams $20. The cops struck me the hardest—I paid two $50 and the rest $20 and $25. But didn't it work beautifully, Mr. Rockwall? And never a rehearsal either! The boys were on time within a fraction of a second. It was two hours before traffic was moving again."

"Thirteen hundred—there you are, Kelly," said Anthony, handing him a check. "Your thousand, and the $300 you were out. You don't despise money, do you, Kelly?"

"Me? said Kelly. I can lick the man who invented poverty."

Anthony called to Kelly when he was at the door. "You didn't notice," he asked, "anywhere in the tie-up, a kind of fat boy without any clothes on shooting arrows around with a bow, did you?"

"Why, no," said Kelly, mystified. "I didn't. If he was like you say, maybe the cops pinched him before I got there."

"I thought the little rascal wouldn't be there," chuckled Anthony. "Goodbye, Kelly."

Moral: Things often aren't as they appear. One cannot always count on luck; occasionally we have to make our own luck.

Based on: O. Henry, "Mammon and the Archer," *The Four Million*

Chapter 5

INDEFATIGABLE / UNSELFISH

The small share of happiness attainable by man exists
only insofar as he is able to cease to think of himself.

Theodore Reik, *Of Love and Lust*

The Salamanna Grapes

There once lived a king with a very beautiful daughter of marriageable age. A neighboring king had three sons, all of whom fell in love with the princess. The princess's father judged all three suitors to be equal and refused to give one preference over the others. He didn't want to be the cause of quarrels among the brothers so he suggested that they travel around the world for six months, and the one who returned with the finest present would become his son-in-law.

The princes set out together, but when the road branched off in three directions, each went his separate way. The older brother traveled for five months without finding anything worth taking home as a present. One morning during the sixth month in a faraway city, he heard a peddler under his window selling fine carpets. When the prince leaned out of the window, he was asked if he wanted to buy a nice carpet. He said that was the last thing he needed; there were carpets all over his palace, even in the kitchen.

The carpet seller argued that the young man did not have a magic carpet like this one. The oldest brother asked what was so special about it. When you step on it, the peddler replied, it takes you great distances through the air. The prince realized that it would be the perfect gift to take to the princess. He paid the asking price of one hundred crowns.

As soon as he stepped onto it, the carpet soared through the air over mountains and valleys and landed at the inn where the brothers had agreed to meet at the end of the six months. The other two had not arrived yet.

The middle brother had also traveled far and wide up to the last days without finding a suitable present. Then he met a peddler selling telescopes who asked if the prince would like to buy one. The young man scoffed that his house was full of fine telescopes, and he didn't need another one.

The telescope seller said that the prince had never seen magic telescopes like these. The brother asked what was so special about them and was told that you could see a hundred miles with them, and even through walls. The middle prince realized that he had found his gift and paid the requested one hundred crowns for the telescope. He took it to the inn and found his older brother. Together they waited for their younger brother.

The youngest brother had found nothing until the last day and had given up all hope. He was on his way home when he heard a fruit vendor selling Salamanna grapes. He had never heard of Salamanna grapes, which didn't grow in his country. He asked the vendor what kind of grapes these were. He was told that they were the finest in the world, and that they worked a special wonder.

The grape vendor told the prince that if someone put a grape in the mouth of a person breathing his or her last, the sick person would get well instantly. The prince was impressed and inquired how much they cost. He was told that they were sold by the grape, and that he would be given a special offer of one hundred crowns per grape. The prince had three hundred crowns in his pocket, so he bought three grapes. He placed them in a small wooden box packed with cotton and went to join his brothers.

When they met at the inn, they shared with one another what they had bought as presents. One of them said that he wondered what was going on at home and at the princess's palace. The middle brother pointed his telescope toward their home city. Everything was as usual. Then he pointed the telescope at their beloved's palace and let out a cry. He could see a stream of carriages there. People were weeping and tearing out their hair. He could see a doctor and a priest at the bedside of the princess. She was still and pale and appeared to be dying. He suggested that they go to her quickly, or it might be too late.

The brothers were fifty miles away and didn't think they could make it in time until the oldest brother invited them to step onto his carpet. The carpet flew directly to the princess's room, passed through the open window, and landed by her bed. The youngest brother took a Salamanna grape from the wooden box and placed it in the mouth of the princess. She swallowed it and opened her eyes immediately. The prince put another grape into her mouth, and she regained her color at once. He gave her the last grape, and she breathed and raised her arms. She was well. She sat up in bed and asked her maids to help her get dressed.

Everyone was rejoicing when the youngest brother announced that he was the winner; without his grapes, the princess would be dead. The middle brother contested this and pointed out that without the telescope, they wouldn't have known that the princess was ill. Therefore, he was the winner. The oldest disagreed with his brothers. He claimed the princess as his bride because without his carpet, they would never have made it to the princess's palace in time to save her.

Thus the quarrels that the king had tried to avoid became even more heated. Finally, the king put an end to their arguing by marrying his daughter to a fourth suitor, who had come to her empty-handed.

Moral: Selfishness, which is not a laudable quality,
       may prevent achievement of desired goals.

Based on: Italo Calvino, "The Salamanna Grapes,"
       Italian Folktales

The Clown of God

One Christmas Eve long ago, a band of strolling players, then called jongleurs, entered a small village in Normandy. A boy led them. Behind him came a strange company dressed in a rainbow of colors. There were a viola player carrying a baby, a sword swallower, a juggler and others; all were dirty and bedraggled. Each performer led one or two lean, weary animals at the end of a leash including a performing bear, a dog, and two monkeys. The chief boxer carried a shivering rabbit under his cloak; a flute player held a scantily feathered rooster.

This poor, tattered band had come to make merry on Christmas Day by performing tricks and dances. Their gay costumes were torn and spattered with mud; the spangles were tarnished and dull. To buy food and clothing, they had only pennies that had been given to them by villagers who had watched them entertain. The villages they had passed through that winter had been very poor. The players had received only a few coppers at each town. The band had always lacked much, but never so much as now.

A great calamity had befallen them. Old Pere Michel had died. He had been very funny, full of quips, jokes, and tricks. When he was their leader, lords and ladies and an occasional duke or princess had watched them perform. Without him, that was no longer so. Neither a lord or lady, nor a duke or a princess would look upon such a sorry company. They had fallen on hard times.

Pere Michel had a merry heart. He had died while standing on his head, playing brass cymbals with his feet. He had neither money, nor jewels, neither lands nor a house to leave behind him, only a few clown's rags—and a son. His wife, Angelique, had died while their child was still an infant. She had been a wandering dancer, very light of foot. Despite her tattered garments, she had been an artist. When her little son took his first steps, he moved so quickly on his feet that everyone knew that he would also be a dancer. He was trained as a jongleur, a baby clown.

Pere Michel's son led the troupe that winter evening, worn and trembling with cold. He had tried to take his father's place since his death, but he was still only a boy. Times were getting harder every day, and it was now Christmas Eve. The village was thronged with people and the inn was full. His Lordship the Bishop was lodged there. Even if it had been empty, the jongleurs would not have been admitted. They were no longer held in high esteem as wandering bands had been in the past.

Even if the innkeeper had welcomed them, the troupe could not afford to stay there. They had scarcely a sou among them. They walked to the end of the village where they found an empty barn, an old stone building. The roof had fallen in, wind came moaning through chinks in the stone, and the straw on the ground was damp, soggy, and foul-smelling. They lodged there.

The trained bear was cold; his fur was matted, and his feet had been cut by sharp cobblestones. He was cross and growled at everyone. The viola player's baby cried continually. Even the monkeys were sullen and whined like unhappy children. The juggler argued with the sword swallower. They were a sorry band of merrymakers.

Pere Michel's son curled up on the straw and tried without success to keep warm. It was a long time before anyone could sleep. Even if all had been quiet, the little jongleur could not have slept. He was too miserable. Finally, the black night began to turn gray, and the stars were dulled by the coming daylight. The boy was so stiff that it hurt to sit up. Pere Michel's son rose and walked out of the barn. He did not know where he was going, but he had to get away, even if it were only briefly. He walked through the narrow streets of the village. No one was stirring. He stopped in front of the little church. It was hardly more than a chapel. No candles had been lighted; the choirboys weren't there yet. As always, the heavy, carved door was unlocked.

Pere Michel's son walked into the small, beautiful church. The stonemason had built well; the woodcarver had clever fingers; the worker in stained glass had made windows that were rich and pure, particularly the round rose window over the altar. The young jongleur stopped before the statue of the Virgin Mary, who, although she held the baby Jesus in her arms, looked sad. The Virgin had good cause to look troubled. Evil days had fallen upon the church and jongleurs alike.

The old priest had died, and a new priest, very serious and very young, had come to take his place. The villagers were indifferent to his sermons and only a few straggled listlessly to Mass. The Bishop had traveled the poor Norman roads to chastise the erring parishioners and perhaps to remove the young priest from his position. The young priest knew this. This was his first church. He had bowed his head and cried bitterly to himself: "Before I have truly begun, oh Lord, I who am thine unworthy servant, have weakly failed."

In the dim light, the Virgin looked sadder than ever. The young jongleur thought that she looked troubled, as he felt. He looked down at his tattered clown's tunic, and he remembered that, as the son of a jongleur and a dancer, he was born to make people laugh. He thought to himself, "Perhaps I can make the heart of our dear Lady lighter." He had nothing to give, but he could do his tricks. Although he was hungry and cold, Pere Michel's son pulled himself to his full height. He was tall for a young boy and as supple as a reed. His tunic, although patched and tarnished was still brightly colored and girdled in green. His jongleur's cap was red. He thought, "If I did my jongleur's work, perhaps it would please Our Lady and be a good thing."

He turned one somersault, and then another and another down the aisle of the church and back again. He seemed small with the light of dawn reflecting off of the high arches of the church. He was like a firefly alone in a deep forest path. He did everything that he had seen Pere Michel do in years past. He was turning a handspring when six solemn choirboys carrying lighted candles walked into the church with the serious young priest and the Bishop in his cope of golden cloth, wearing his miter and carrying his jeweled crozier. The Bishop demanded of the boy, "How darest thou profane the house of God with thine unholy tumbling?"

Pere Michel's son replied: "Oh, Monseigneur, I cannot speak the word of God to comfort the people as you can. I cannot read from big books as can the priest. I do not know my letters. I cannot sing as can the choirboys. But, oh, Monseigneur, I can dance, and such wonderful tricks have I played for Our Lady! I pray you let me dance again. A man must do what he can on Christmas Day in the morning."

The young priest spoke: "Monseigneur, you remember the words:

>Praise Him with the sound of the trumpet.
>Praise Him with the psaltery and harp.
>Praise Him with timbrel and dance.
>• • • • • • • • • • •
>Let everything that hath breath praise the Lord.
>Praise ye the Lord.

It is said that the text had its origin in the days when men danced within the temple before the Holy of Holies. What harm can the clown do? He has an honest desire."

Pere Michel's son waited only for the priest's words. In an instant he was turning a cartwheel across the church and back again. In a blur of colors, red, white, and green, he was going round and round. He looked like the rose window above the altar—as if it had suddenly began to move across the dim church. So moves the sun across a darkening sky.

By this time the church was filled with people, who were breathless with amazement. Next, the jongleur began to dance on his half-frozen feet. Movement flowed through him, rippling from his outstretched fingers down to his toes. The children were enthralled. They asked, "Has he borrowed feathers from a rooster's tail that he may dance so lightly?"

Then Pere Michel's son stood still. His heart was pounding like a hammer on an anvil. He stood on his hands before the Virgin. At first he swung his heels back and forth jauntily; then slowly he brought his feet together above his head until they were pointed like the arch of the church windows. The children cried, "See, he is praying with his feet!" He did look as though he were praying.

At this trick the Bishop's miter trembled; his crozier shook with wrath. He thundered: "Go! Profane this church no longer."

When the young priest saw the anger of the Bishop, he said to the boy, "Come with me, mon petit jongleur de Dieu. Come with me, my little clown of God!" The young priest named him that because years before, the good St. Francis, as he went singing along the roads near Assisi, called himself and his followers "Joculatores Domini," jongleurs, or minstrels, of God.

The priest saw that Pere Michel's son had a very red nose, not only because it was painted so, but because it was nearly frozen. He saw that his face was not only white from chalk but pale from hunger and drawn by weariness. He led the clown out of the church, through the carved door. They were a strange sight, the serious priest in his black cassock, the boy with his face painted and his gay clown's rags. The little jongleur looked up to the priest with troubled, questioning eyes and asked, "My band, my poor folk, they are cold, and they are starving in an old barn. What can I do?"

"Fear not, my son," the priest said. "My father left me a small patrimony, and in the name of Her whom we serve, you and your band shall be cared for."

They had not gone far before a shout was heard from the church. The children cried out: "She is smiling—the Virgin! It is a miracle. The jongleur made her laugh. She smiles. Our Lady smiles!" The children spoke the truth. For the first time, in the warm candlelight, the people in the church noticed a curve in the Virgin's lips. Pere Michel's son had actually made the statue smile. From that day, the village was called the Village of the Smiling Virgin. From then onward the villagers always went to Mass when the young priest called them. They followed him all his life as sheep follow their shepherd. They had seen a miracle with their own eyes! The young priest had done a kindness to the weary band and to the boy who had brought joy to the Virgin!

Thus did the jongleurs tell the old tale. Even these days, people still speak of Pere Michel's son and of his wonderful dance before the Virgin in the early Christmas dawn, because as he said, "A man must do what he can—on Christmas Day in the morning."

Moral: It is right to give, even if you don't have much to share.
Helping others is its own reward.

Based on: Katherine Gibson, "The Clown of God,"
The Golden Bird and Other Stories

The Indian Cinderella

Years ago a great Indian warrior lived on the shores of a wide bay
on the North Atlantic coast. He was one of the best friends and
helpers of Glooskap, a god of the Eastern Woodlands Indians, and
had done many good deeds. This warrior had a very wonderful and
strange power: he could make himself invisible. He could mingle
unseen among his enemies and listen to their plotting.

He was known among the Eastern Woodlands people as Strong
Wind, the Invisible. He lived with his sister in a lodge near the
ocean. His sister was very helpful to him in his work. Many maidens wanted to marry him. He was much sought after because of his
great deeds. Strong Wind said that he would marry the first maiden
who could see him as he came home at night. Many made the
attempt, but it was a long time before one succeeded.

Strong Wind used a clever trick to test the truthfulness of those
maidens who sought to win him. Each evening at dusk, his sister
walked on the beach with any girl who wished to make the trial. His
sister could always see him, but no one else could. As he returned
home in the twilight, his sister would see him approaching and ask
the girl who sought him if she saw him. Each girl would answer
falsely, "Yes." Then his sister would ask what he was using to draw
his sled. Each girl would answer: moose hide, a pole, or a great
cord. Then his sister would know that they all had lied. Their
answers were mere guesses.

A great chief who lived in the village had three daughters. Their
mother had long been dead. One of the daughters was much
younger than the others. She was very beautiful, gentle, and widely loved. Her sisters were very jealous of her and treated her cruel-
ly. They clothed her in rags, cut off her long black hair, and burned
her face with coals from the fire to disfigure her. Then they lied to
their father, telling him that she had done these things to herself.
Nevertheless, the young girl kept her heart gentle and went will-

ingly about her work.

The chief's two older daughters, like the other maidens in the tribe, tried to win Strong Wind. One evening, as the sun went down, they walked along the shore with Strong Wind's sister and waited for him to return. Soon he came home from his day's work, pulling his sled. His sister asked them if they could see her brother. They said that they could. Then his sister asked of what material his shoulder strap was made. Both said that it was made of rawhide.

The sisters entered Strong Wind's lodge, where they hoped they could see him eating his supper. When he took off his coat and moccasins, they could see them although they could not see him. Strong Wind knew that they had lied. He kept himself from their sight, and they went home disappointed.

One day the chief's youngest daughter with her rags and her burned face decided to seek Strong Wind. She patched her clothes with bits of birch bark, put on the few ornaments that she possessed, and went to look for the Invisible One as the other girls of the village had done. Her sisters laughed at her and told her that she was foolish. As she walked along the road, people laughed at her because of her tattered clothing and her scarred face. She ignored them and continued on her way.

Strong Wind's sister received the young girl kindly and at twilight took her to the beach. Soon Strong Wind came home, drawing his sled. His sister asked the maiden if she saw him, and she admitted that she didn't. The sister asked the young woman again if she saw her brother. This time the maiden said that she did, and that he was very handsome. The sister asked her with what he was pulling his sled. The young woman answered, "With the rainbow." Then the sister asked of what his bowstring was made. The maiden answered, "His bowstring is the Milky Way."

Strong Wind's sister knew that because the maiden had spoken the truth at first, her brother had made himself visible to her. When she knew that the young woman had seen her brother, she took her home and bathed her. All the scars disappeared from her face and her hair grew long and black again. Strong Wind's sister gave the young woman fine clothes to wear and many rich ornaments. Then she asked the maiden to take the wife's seat in the lodge. Soon Strong Wind entered, sat beside her, and called her his bride. They were married the next day, and she helped him accomplish his many good deeds.

The young woman's two older sisters were very upset when they heard what had happened. Strong Wind, who knew of their cruelty, resolved to punish them. He turned them both into aspen trees and rooted them in the earth. Since that time the leaves of the aspen have always trembled, and they shiver in fear at the approach of Strong Wind. It doesn't matter how softly he comes, they are still aware of his great power and anger because of their lies and cruelty to their sister long ago.

Moral: Deceit will eventually be discovered. Treat others
      as you would have them treat you.

Based on: Cyrus Macmillan, "The Indian Cinderella,"
          Canadian Wonder Tales

A New York Merchant's Way to Wealth

Alexander Turney Stewart, the great nineteenth-century merchant, was an enigma to many of his fellow citizens. They had difficulty understanding how a young Irish immigrant with little capital and no training in the dry goods business could have achieved such outstanding success in the most competitive industry of his day. Women of the city and the surrounding region flocked to his stores and made him a millionaire before he was thirty-five years old.

Stewart's own explanation—that his success was due wholly to rigid adherence to a few business policies, most of which were derived from the Golden Rule—was too simplistic for his peers. They insisted on finding some explanation for his success other than hard work and an ethical business policy. They claimed that Stewart never had intended to enter the dry goods business, but had been forced into it by circumstances beyond his control at a time when he was ignorant even of the most common trade terms.

Others contended that Stewart had already formulated his progressive policies when he opened his store at 283 Broadway, his first store. Observers in this camp told the following anecdotes.

One of Stewart's clerks told a customer that a piece of calico was of a high quality, that the colors were "fast" and would not wash out, and if they did, the material could be returned and the purchase price would be refunded. The remarks were overheard by Stewart, who asked the clerk how he could tell a customer something that he knew to be untrue. The clerk, surprised by being called to account, replied that the woman would not return the goods, and if she did she could easily be put off by being told that she must be mistaken, that the purchase must have been made at another store.

Stewart reminded the clerk that he had told a lie to make a sale. He made it clear that no sales must be made in his store or in his name that involved misrepresentation. The clerk was told that he could either comply with that policy or resign.

One day in his Greenwich Street shop, Stewart heard a salesman tell an older woman that the calico in front of her had cost twenty-five cents a yard, but that he would sell it to her for twenty cents. Pleased, the woman purchased the material and left. Stewart asked the salesman if it were necessary to lie to conduct their business. The salesman said that he did it only with accomplished shoppers who were in the habit of beating down the price. Stewart told him never to practice that in the store again.

Many of Stewart's contemporaries believed that he held superstitious beliefs. One of them believed that Stewart's great success had occurred because the first customer at his Broadway store had brought him luck. According to this anecdote, a young lady whose acquaintance Stewart had made said to him on the day before the opening of his first store that he must not sell anything until she came in and made the first purchase, because she would bring him luck. True to her promise, she drove up in her carriage early the next day and purchased two hundred dollars worth of goods, principally Irish laces.

Many years passed, and the lady married and moved to a city in Europe. Once when Stewart was in that city on business, he learned that his first customer was still living there, but in much reduced circumstances. Her husband had died, but not before squandering her fortune.

Stewart acquired a nice apartment and furnished it in the style to which his acquaintance had been accustomed. He called upon her and renewed their acquaintance. After talking about old times and old friends, he asked to take her for a ride in his carriage. After taking in the sights of the city, he drove her to the apartment and told her that if she approved, it was her new home. He provided her with an annuity for the remainder of her life. She lived not only in comfort but in affluence, supported entirely by him.

Another anecdote about Stewart's alleged superstition involved an old apple woman who had a stand outside his third Broadway store. Reputedly, the merchant thought that she brought him luck, and in fact his greatest success in the New York dry goods business was achieved at that location. When he opened his most opulent store at Broadway and Reade Street, he personally moved the apple lady's stand to the new store to ensure that her lucky influence continued at the new location.

Sixteen years after the opening of the Reade Street store, he opened another store at Broadway and Tenth Street. Again, he personally moved the apple lady's stand to the new store. The reason he gave for doing this was his belief that when she died or left the front of the store, his good luck would go with her.

Eventually, the apple lady died, and Stewart's premonition came true. A few months after her death, Stewart's health began to fail. The memory of the apple lady was hardly forgotten before the merchant was in his grave.

Moral: Hard work and sound business principles are important, but luck also helps to achieve success.

Based on: Tristam Potter Coffin and Hennig Cohen, "A New York Merchant's Way to Wealth," *The Parade of Heroes*

The Gift of the Magi

One dollar and eighty-seven cents. That was all, and sixty cents of it was in pennies. Pennies saved one and two at a time by shaving a penny off the bill with the grocer, the vegetable man, and the butcher. Della counted it three times. It was still only one dollar and eighty-seven cents, and tomorrow was Christmas Day.

There was clearly nothing to do but flop down on the threadbare little couch and cry. So Della did that. Why is life made up of sobs, sniffles, and smiles, with sniffles dominating? She looked around and saw a shabby furnished apartment rented for eight dollars a week.

In the vestibule was a letter-box into which no letter would go and an electric button from which no mortal finger could coax a ring. Next to the doorbell was a card bearing the name "Mr. James Dillingham Young." The "Dillingham" had been added to the card when its possessor was earning thirty dollars a week. Now that he was earning only twenty dollars a week, it should probably be reduced to an unassuming "D." When Mr. James Dillingham Young came home and entered his apartment, he was called "Jim" and always lovingly hugged by Mrs. James Dillingham Young, also known as Della.

Della finished her cry and dried her cheeks. Tomorrow was Christmas Day, and she only had a dollar and eighty-seven cents to buy Jim a present. She had been saving for months. Twenty dollars a week didn't go very far. Expenses had been greater than she had anticipated. She had hoped to get something nice for him, something worthy of the honor of being owned by Jim.

Della looked into the mirror. Her eyes were shining brilliantly, but her face had lost its color. Quickly she pulled down her hair and let it fall to its full length. The James Dillingham Youngs had two possessions in which they took pride. One was Jim's gold pocket watch, which had been his father's and his grandfather's. The other was Della's hair.

Della's beautiful hair fell about her, rippling and shining like a brown cascade. It reached her knees and almost made a garment for her. Then she did it up again nervously. A tear or two splashed on the worn red carpet. She put on her old brown jacket and her old brown hat and went out the door and down the stairs to the street.

Della walked down the street and stopped at the sign: "Madame Sofronie. Hair Goods of All Kinds." She hurried up one flight and inquired of the proprietress, "Will you buy my hair?"

Madame said, "I buy hair. Take off your hat and let me look at it." Down rippled the brown cascade. Madame lifted the mass with a practiced hand and said, "Twenty dollars." Della agreed with that amount, and the deed was done.

For the next two hours Della visited many stores looking for Jim's present. Finally she found it. It looked as though it had been made for Jim and no one else. She had turned all the stores in the area inside out, and there was no other like it anywhere. It was a platinum fob chain, simple and uncluttered in design. It proclaimed its value by substance and not by ornamentation—as all good things should. It was worthy of The Watch. As soon as Della saw it, she knew that it must be Jim's. It was like him. Quietness and quality—the description applied to both.

Della paid twenty-one dollars for it and hurried home with eighty-seven cents left over. With that chain on his watch Jim could be proud in any company. Grand as his watch was, he occasionally looked at it on the sly because of the old leather strap he used in place of a chain.

When Della reached home she got out her curling iron and went to work repairing the ravages made by generosity added to love. Soon her head was covered with tiny, loose-lying curls that made her look like a truant schoolboy. She took a long, critical look at her reflection in the mirror. She thought, "If Jim doesn't kill me before he takes a second look at me, he'll say I look like a Coney Island chorus girl. But what could I have done with a dollar and eighty-seven cents?"

By seven o'clock the coffee had been made and the dinner was being kept warm on the back of the stove. Jim was never late. Della held the fob chain in her hand and sat on the corner of the table near the door through which he always entered. She had a habit of saying silent little prayers about everyday things. When she heard his step on the stairs, she prayed, "Please God, make him think I am still pretty."

The door opened and Jim stepped in and closed it. He looked very serious. He needed a new overcoat and was without gloves. He stopped inside the door with his eyes fixed on Della with an expression she could not read. It was not anger, surprise, disapproval, horror, nor any of the sentiments she had expected. He simply stared her with that peculiar expression on his face.

Della walked over to him and said, "Jim. darling, don't look at me that way. I had my hair cut off and sold it because I couldn't have lived through Christmas without giving you a present. It'll grow out again—you won't mind, will you? I just had to do it. My hair grows awfully fast. You don't know what a beautiful gift I've got for you."

"You've cut off your hair?" asked Jim, as if he had not yet arrived at that fact.

"Cut it off and sold it," said Della. "Don't you like me just as well, anyhow? I'm me without my hair, aren't I?"

Jim looked around the room curiously. "You say your hair is gone?" he asked.

"You needn't look for it," said Della. "It's sold, I tell you—sold and gone, too. It's Christmas Eve. Be good to me; it went for you."

Jim seemed to awaken from his trance. He hugged Della. The Magi had brought valuable gifts to the newborn Christ, but they were not gifts with sacrifice, as hers was. Jim drew a package from his overcoat pocket and placed it on the table.

Jim said, "Don't get me wrong, Della. A haircut couldn't make me like my girl any less. If you'll unwrap that package you'll see what had me going at first." Nimble fingers tore at the string and paper. Then an ecstatic scream of joy was followed by a quick change to tears and hysterical wails, requiring all the comforting powers that the lord of the apartment could muster.

For there lay The Combs—the set of combs that Della had worshiped for a long time in a window on Broadway. They were beautiful combs, pure tortoiseshell with jewelled rims—just the shade to wear in the beautiful brown hair that had vanished. She knew that they were expensive combs, and she had yearned over them without the slightest hope of ever possessing them. Now they were hers, but the tresses that should have held the coveted adornments were gone. She hugged the combs to her bosom, looked at Jim, and again reminded him how fast her hair grew.

Suddenly Della jumped up and extended Jim's present to him in her open palm. The precious metal seemed to reflect her ardent spirit. She said, "Isn't it a dandy, Jim? I hunted all over town to find it. You'll have to look at the time a hundred times a day now. Give me your watch. I want to see how it looks on it."

Instead of doing as she asked, Jim sat down on the couch and put his hands under the back of his head and smiled. He said, "Dell, let's put our Christmas presents away and keep them awhile. They're too nice to use just now. I sold the watch to get the money to buy your combs. Why don't you put the dinner on."

The Magi were wise men who brought gifts to the Babe in the manger. They invented the art of giving Christmas presents. Their gifts were no doubt wise ones. This has been the story of two young people who sacrificed for each other the greatest treasures of their house. Of all who give and receive gifts, these two are the wisest. They are the Magi.

Moral: Generous giving provides more satisfaction than receiving.

Based on: O. Henry, "The Gift of the Magi," *The Four Million*

Chapter 6

RESOLUTE / COURAGEOUS

In life's small things be resolute and great
To keep thy muscle trained; know'st thou when fate
Thy measure takes, or when she'll say to thee,
"I find thee worthy to do this deed for me."

James Russell Lowell, *Sayings, No. 1*

Citizen William Tell

Centuries ago, men came out of the valleys around Lake Lucerne in the heart of the Swiss Alps to forge an alliance and to swear loyalty to it. The Switzerland of today grew out of that alliance. The inhabitants of those valleys fought many fierce battles against the powerful foreign lords of their land, the ruling nobles and princes, before freedom was won. One of the bravest fighters for the freedom of Switzerland was William Tell.

William Tell was a chamois hunter, a quiet man who usually shunned the society of his fellows. He lived near Altdorf in the canton of Uri. When hunting chamois, Tell carried his bow on his back. He seldom missed a shot; he was the best bowman in the valley. He sold his chamois skins to the market in Lucerne and with his earnings lived a humble, contented, and secluded life with his family.

Gessler, the tyrannical Austrian bailiff of Uri, ruled with an iron hand. Tension had existed between the Swiss and the Austrians since long before 1315, when a Swiss force defeated the large Austrian army advancing from Zug to Schwyz at Morgarten, laying the foundations of Swiss liberty.

One day Gessler thought of a new way to antagonize the free peasants who resisted his rule. He directed his men to place a hat on top of a pole in the marketplace of Altdorf. He ordered that every grown man that walked by it must kneel down and pay homage to the hat, as if it were the bailiff or the Emperor himself. Two armed soldiers were assigned to guard the pole and the hat and to enforce the bailiff's order. Villagers went out of their way to avoid walking by the hat.

This order of the bailiff, to kneel down before an empty hat, filled the people with indignation. On November 8, 1307, the leaders of the three cantons, or forest districts, around Lake Lucerne met one night on the Rutli, a lonely pasture in the forest above the lake, to make a plan to rid themselves of their foreign oppressors and set their country free. Werner von Stauffacher of Schwyz, Walter Furst of Uri, and Arnold von Melchthal of Unterwalden, each with ten companions, including William Tell, met to form the plan. They agreed to storm the fortresses after dark on the coming New Year's Eve to drive out the bailiffs.

One day soon after these meetings, William Tell came into the marketplace of Altdorf, holding his bow in his right hand and his son with his left hand. The men of Uri admired him as a fellow citizen and a champion archer. Tell walked by the hat on the pole without kneeling. The two guards seized him and told him he would go to prison for disobeying the bailiff's order. He thrust the guards aside and told them that he was a free man. He knelt before God, he bowed his head before the Emperor and his representatives, but he would not pay homage to an empty hat.

At that moment Gessler entered the square with a retinue of several dozen heavily armed soldiers. The citizens of Altdorf came into the marketplace to support Tell. Tell told them to stay calm and not to get into trouble over him. Many of those who had sworn the oath at Rutli were there. Tell and Gessler faced each other in silence. Gessler hated Tell, one of the leaders of the free men opposing his plans.

Gessler ordered Tell to be thrown in prison for disobeying his orders. Tell responded that the citizens were free men, and that they didn't have to pay reverence to an empty hat. Gessler saw that Tell carried his bow with him, which was against the law. Gessler told Tell that he would be punished for being armed.

Gessler commanded his guards, "Seize Tell's son and stand him under the linden tree. Place this apple on the boy's head and measure eighty paces away from him. You, Tell, draw your bow. You are to shoot the apple off the boy's head. If you hit your mark, I will let you go free. If you miss the mark, then you shall die, both you and your son."

Tell looked at Gessler with horror in his eyes. Rage seized him; he wanted to rush at the bailiff and drag him off his horse. Then he thought of his son. The threat of death was hanging over his head too. He forced himself to kneel down and to ask the bailiff's pardon. He said, "I am a simple man. It was not out of ill will that I disobeyed your order. Forgive me, and let me go." The boy's grandfather also stepped forward, kneeled before the hated tyrant, and pleaded on behalf of his son. The bailiff was not moved.

Gessler's men positioned Tell's son under the linden tree and began to blindfold him. The boy refused the blindfold, telling them that he was not afraid of his father's arrow. Tell took aim. A deadly silence fell over the entire square. Tell dropped his arm holding the bow and said that he could not do it.

The bailiff looked at him mockingly. He told Tell that if he could carry arms illegally and disobey his order to kneel before the hat, then he could so this, too. The bailiff reminded him that if he didn't shoot, both he and his son would die.

An uncanny calm took possession of Tell. He measured the distance between himself and the boy and then between himself and Gessler. He placed one arrow into position in his bow and took a second arrow out of his quiver and stuck it in his belt. He took aim and shot the arrow. It split the apple in half. A thousand townspeople shouted with delight. The valley folk embraced one another with joy. They began to carry Tell away.

Gessler ordered his men to drive the people back. He congratulated Tell that it had been a master shot and asked what the purpose of the second arrow was. Tell hesitated until the bailiff assured him that whatever he had to say, his life was not at stake. Tell then answered that the second arrow was for Gessler; if he had missed the apple and killed this own child, the bailiff would have been the next target. Tell said that he wouldn't have missed.

Gessler turned pale. He directed his men to put Tell in chains and said, "Take him to my fortress at Kussnacht. The walls there are more than three feet thick. He shall lie in the deepest dungeon and never see the sun or moonlight again. He shall live on but in such a life that he would rather be dead. I will see to it that I am safe from his arrows." The boy clung to his father's arm and begged him not to go. The grandfather had to drag the boy away from his father. The old man's heart was broken. Tell showed no fear.

Gessler's boat was waiting in the harbor. It was the bailiff's official boat with eight pairs of oars. Tell was flung down in the middle of the boat; he was chained and well guarded. Gessler thought that Tell would never be able to harm him again. Gessler and his soldiers rowed out into the lake, which was surrounded by mountains and ravines.

Tell looked up at the sky. A bank of clouds was moving in from the south. He knew what that meant: a foehn, a warm, unhealthy wind that brought sudden storms. The air was heavy, and gradually the sky grew dark. Suddenly violent gusts of wind blew out onto the lake from the valleys. The gusts whipped up the waves, which struck the boat with increasing force. Two oars splintered like matchsticks. The tremendous waves jerked the helm out of the steersman's hands, and the boat rocked back and forth at the mercy of the storm.

Gessler and his men were pale with fear. They were afraid that the boat might be shattered into fragments on the rocks. The helmsman turned to the bailiff and said, "We are in great danger. We have lost control of the boat. There is only one hope for us and that lies with Tell. With his great strength and experience, he might be able to hold the helm. Let him be unchained so that he can help us."

Tell was unfettered and took the helm. He told the oarsmen to row with their utmost strength. He promised that the lake would be calmer on the other side of the large rock ledge extending out into the lake toward which he was steering. The oarsmen took heart again and rowed with all their might. Finally the boat reached the small peninsula of rock.

Tell knew it well. A flat rock ten feet wide ran out from it just above the level of the water. In later years, this rock became known as Tell's Platte. Great waves were breaking over the rock. Tell's face was rigid. He grasped the helm firmly and jammed it back, causing the boat to jerk around violently and face the open lake. He grabbed his bow and arrows and leaped out of the boat onto the flat rock.

Gessler sprang from his seat but was thrown down again by a large wave. Tell plunged into the thick undergrowth and was quickly out of sight. Without a helmsman, the boat tossed helplessly on the waters.

Tell knew that Gessler would try to land at Brunnen, a nearby village on the lake, and that he would ride from there to his fortress at Kussnacht. Tell knew all the trails and footpaths and wound his way through the forest until he was within sight of Brunnen and the canton of Schwyz. He stopped to eat at the Sust Tavern in Brunnen and heard that the bailiff's boat had survived the storm and landed at the village dock. It was time to act.

Tell chose a footpath that led through the thick forest. He walked all night and by morning was near the only approach to the bailiff's fortress, a deep, narrow gorge with thick shrubs on both sides of the trail. There he hid and waited for the bailiff. Eventually he saw Gessler. Tell drew his bow and shot a arrow that pierced the bailiff's heart. Gessler's last sight was Tell standing tall above him. Tell evaded Gessler's men and headed for home.

The news traveled fast to the canton of Uri that the bailiff was dead and could no longer ravage the country or torment the peasants. The men of Uri crowded into the streets of the small towns and discussed the events with unsuppressed excitement. When Tell entered Altdorf, his friends flocked around him and greeted him with shouts of joy as their rescuer and deliverer. He left the crowds, with his wife at his side, to return home.

On the morning of New Year's Day, 1308, Tell got up at dawn and climbed the hills to hunt chamois. From the heights, he looked down on Altdorf. Where the fortress had stood the day before, smoke was now rising from a heap of ruins.

The people of Altdorf had left few stones of the fortress standing. William Tell's deed had been a signal to the men from the other cantons to begin their fight for freedom. They stormed the other fortresses and drove the Emperor's representatives out of the country.

The three cantons set up a common system of law and administration. They vowed never to submit to a foreign judge or overlord and to support each other with life-and-death loyalty. The Switzerland of today grew out of the old Deeds of Confederation, drawn up by the three valley cantons and the cantons that joined them.

After William Tell died, the men of Uri came to Tell's house and asked for his bow. They said, "This shall be kept forever and handed down to our children and grandchildren. It shall remind us that courage, daring, and selfless devotion laid the foundation of our Confederation, and that these things have made it strong." Over time citizen William Tell became a national hero of the Swiss people.

Moral: The collective good cannot be obtained without courage and determination among those allied to the cause.

Based on: Fritz Muller-Guggenbuhl, "William Tell and the Swiss Confederation," *Swiss-Alpine Folk-Tales*

The Bravery of Arnold von Winkelried

The union of the cantons and cities of the republic of Switzerland has been a remarkable facet of history. Of different races, languages, and religions—unalike in habits, tastes, opinions, and costumes—they have, nevertheless, held together by pressure from without, and a spirit of patriotism has kept the mountainous republic whole for centuries.

Originally the lands had been fiefs of the Holy Roman Empire. The Emperor was the lord of the cities. The great family of Hapsburg, who became hereditary rulers of the Empire, were in reality Swiss; the county that gave them their title was in the canton of Aargau. Rodolf of Hapsburg was elected leader of the burghers of Zurich long before he was chosen to lead the Empire. He remained Swiss at heart, retaining his mountaineer's open simplicity and honesty to the end of his life. The country was loyal and prosperous during his reign.

Unfortunately, his son Albert permitted those tyrannies of his bailiffs that goaded the Swiss to their celebrated revolt and began the long series of wars with the House of Hapsburg—or, as it was called later, Austria—that finally established Switzerland's independence.

On one side the Dukes of Austria, with their ponderous German chivalry, wanted to reduce the cantons and cities of the Swiss to vassalage, not to the Imperial Crown, a distant and scarcely felt obligation, but to the Duchy of Austria. On the other side, the hardy Swiss peasants and sturdy burghers understood their true position: Austrian control would expose their young men to fighting in the Dukes' wars, cause demands to be made on their property, and fill their hills with castles for ducal bailiffs who would be no more than licensed robbers. It was not surprising that the generations of William Tell and Arnold von Winkelried bequeathed a resolute purpose of resistance to their descendants.

In 1386, many years after the first assertion of Swiss independence, Leopold the Handsome, Duke of Austria, a bold but overly proud and violent prince, involved himself in a quarrel with the Swiss concerning insulting tolls and tributes imposed upon the cities near the Austrian border. A bitter war broke out, and men of the Swiss city of Lucerne attacked the customhouse at Rothenburg, where the tolls had been particularly heavy. Lucerne admitted the cities of Sempach and Richensee to their league.

Leopold and all the neighboring nobles joined forces. They were spurred on by their hatred and contempt for the Swiss, whom they considered low-born and presumptuous. In one day the Duke received twenty pledges of support in his march against Sempach and Lucerne. He sent Johann Bonstetten with a large force in the direction of Zurich and led his own men, mounted and on foot, to advance on Sempach. Zurich undertook its own defense, and the forest cantons sent their brave peasants to support Lucerne and Sempach.

Leopold's troops rode around the walls of Sempach, hurling insults at the inhabitants. Leopold taunted Sempach with the reckless destruction his men caused by destroying the surrounding fields. He shouted, "Send a breakfast to the reapers." From the city walls, the burgomaster pointed to the woods in the distance where his allies were hiding and answered, "My masters of Lucerne and their friends will bring it."

The Duke's wiser friends, including the Baron von Hasenberg, suggested waiting until they were joined by the troops of Bonstetten, who had gone towards Zurich. This prudent counsel was ignored by the younger knights, who boasted that they would deliver up this handful of villains by noon.

The story of that July 9, 1386, battle was told by one of the burghers named Tchudi, who fought in the ranks of Lucerne. He was a brave warrior and a storyteller. His ballad was translated by another storyteller, Sir Walter Scott:

> And thus to each other said,
> Yon handful down to hew
> Will be no boastful tale to tell,
> The peasants are so few.

The Duke's men were drawn up in a solid, compact body, presenting an unbroken line of spears that projected beyond their wall of shields and polished armor. The Swiss were not only few in number, but armor was scarce among them. Some had boards fastened on their arms as shields, and some had halberds that had been used by their forefathers at the battle of Morgarten in 1315, which had laid the foundations of Swiss liberty. Still others had two-handed swords and battle-axes. The Swiss drew themselves up in the shape of a wedge.

> The gallant Swiss confederates then
> They prayed to God aloud,
> And He displayed His rainbow fair,
> Against a swarthy cloud.

The villagers rushed against the tightly packed spears of the Austrians, but in vain. The banner of Lucerne was in the most danger. Their leader was killed along with sixty of his men, and no Austrians had been wounded. The flanks of the Austrians began to advance to enclose the small peasant force and destroy it. In a moment of danger and stillness, a voice was heard. Arnold von Winkelried of Unterwalden, with the determination of a man who dares all things, saw the only way to save his country and shouted, "I will open a passage."

> I have a virtuous wife at home,
> A wife and infant son.
> I leave them to my country's care
> The field shall yet be won!
> He rushed against the Austrian band
> In desperate career,
> And with his body, breast, and hand,
> Bore down each hostile spear
> Four lances splintered on his crest,
> Six shivered in his side,
> Still the serried files he pressed,
> He broke their ranks and died!

The very weight of the desperate charge of this courageous man opened a breach in the line of spears. In rushed the Swiss wedge, and the weight of the Austrian nobles' armor and the length of their spears were only an encumbrance. They began to fall before the Swiss blows, and Duke Leopold was urged to flee. He said, "I would rather die honorably than live with dishonor."

Leopold saw his standard-bearer struck to the ground and seized the banner and waved it over his head. He threw himself into the thickest throng of his enemy. His body was found among a heap of dead soldiers. No less than 2,000 of his force died with him, of whom a third were counts, barons, and knights.

> Then lost was banner, spear, and shield
> At Sempach in the flight;
> The cloister vaults at Konigsfeld
> Hold many an Austrian knight.

The Swiss lost only 200, but, since they were tired from the heat of the July sun, they did not pursue their enemy. They gave thanks to the God of victories, and the next day they buried the dead. They carried Duke Leopold and twenty-seven of his most illustrious companions to the Abbey of Konigsfeld. They buried him in the old tomb of his forefathers, the lords of Aargau, who had been interred there in the days before the House of Hapsburg had grown arrogant with success.

Every July 9, Swiss people assemble on the battlefield around four stone crosses that mark the site. A priest gives a thanksgiving sermon on the victory that ensured the freedom of Switzerland, and another reads the roll of the brave 200, who, after Winkelried's example, gave their lives for the cause. The congregation then proceeds to a small battle-chapel, the walls of which are painted with the deed of Arnold von Winkelried and the distinguished achievements of other confederates. Masses are said for the slain. It is not surprising that men nurtured in the memory of such actions were among the most trusted soldiery in Europe, for example, the Swiss guards at the Vatican.

Moral: One man or woman can make a difference, especially when that person is completely unselfish.

Based on: Charlotte Mary Yonge, "The Battle of Sempach," *A Book of Golden Deeds of All Times and All Lands*

The Legend of the Arabian Astrologer

Many hundreds of years ago, a Moorish king named Aben Habuz reigned over the kingdom of Granada. In his younger days he had led a life of constant warring and plunder. Now the old conqueror had grown old and feeble. He desired nothing more than to live at peace with the world and to enjoy the possessions he had taken from his neighbors.

Unfortunately this peace-loving old monarch had young rivals to contend with: princes full of his earlier passion for fame and fighting who wanted to even the scores he had run up with their fathers. Certain remote districts of his own territories that he had treated high-handedly in his younger days also rebelled against him. He had foes on every side; also, since Granada was surrounded by wild and craggy mountains that hid the approach of the enemy, Aben Habuz was kept in a constant state of vigilance. He did not know from what direction hostile forces might come.

In vain, Aben Habuz built watchtowers in the mountains and stationed guards at every pass. His foes ravaged his lands beneath his very nose and made off with loot and prisoners into the mountains. While Aben Habuz was being harassed by these raiders, an ancient Arabian astrologer arrived at his court. Ibrahim Ebn Abu Ayub had traveled most of the way from Egypt on foot. He was said to have lived ever since the days of Mohammed and to be the son of Abu Ayub, the last of the companions of the Prophet. As a child, he had followed the army of Amru into Egypt, where for many years Ibrahim had studied the dark sciences, particularly magic, among the Egyptian priests. It was said that he had found the secret of prolonging life.

This wonderful old man was entertained by the king, who offered him an apartment in the palace. The astrologer preferred to live in a cave in the side of the hill that rose above the city of Granada, the hill upon which the Alhambra was later built. He enlarged the cave to form a spacious and lofty hall, with a circular hole at the top through which he could see the heavens and the stars even at midday. The walls were covered with Egyptian hieroglyphics with cabalistic symbols and with sketches of the stars and their signs. He furnished the hall with many implements, fabricated by the clever artificers of Granada under his direction. Their occult properties were known only to him.

Within a short time the sage Ibrahim became a trusted counselor of the king, who asked him for advice in all things. One day Aben Habuz complained to the sage of the restless vigilance he had to maintain against the encroachments of his neighbors. The astrologer remained silent for awhile and then replied, "When I was in Egypt, I saw a great marvel devised by an old pagan priestess.

On a mountain above the city of Borsa, overlooking the great valley of the Nile, was the figure of a ram and above it the figure of a cock, both made of brass and turning on a pivot. Whenever the city was threatened with invasion, the ram would turn in the direction of the threat, and the cock would crow. The inhabitants of the city were informed of the danger and the direction from which it was coming and could take the necessary precautions to defend themselves."

Aben Habuz exclaimed, "What a treasure such a ram would be to keep an eye on the mountains around me and then such a cock to crow in time of danger. How securely I would sleep in my palace with such sentinels on the mountain!"

The sage added that he had remained among the priests studying the rites and ceremonies of their idolatrous faith, seeking to master the hidden knowledge for which they were known. One day when Ibrahim was sitting on the banks of the Nile, talking with an ancient priest, the priest pointed to the pyramids and told him that all he could teach him was nothing compared with the knowledge locked up in those mighty monuments.

The priest told Ibrahim of a wondrous book of knowledge, containing all the secrets of magic and art, buried in a sepulchral chamber in the central pyramid. The book had been handed down from generation to generation to King Solomon. When Ibrahim heard this, he knew that he had to get possession of that book. He paid many soldiers and Egyptian workers to help him penetrate the sepulchral chamber in the very heart of the central pyramid. He found the precious book, and, seizing it with trembling hands, groped his way out of the hidden passages.

Aben Habuz asked the astrologer of what use the book of knowledge was to him. Ibrahim replied that the book instructed him in all magic arts and could command the assistance of supernatural beings to accomplish his plans. The sage added that the Talisman of Borsa was familiar to him, permitting him to do many things, such as providing the king with safeguards against attack. Aben Habuz promised Ibrahim the riches of the treasury if he could provide such a safeguard.

The astrologer immediately erected a great tower atop the royal palace. In the upper part of the tower was a circular hall with windows facing every point of the compass. In front of each window was a table on which were arranged, as on a chessboard, replicas of an army of cavalry and infantry, with the representation of the leader that ruled in that direction, all carved of wood. To each table was attached a small lance on which was engraved Chaldaic characters. This hall was always kept locked.

On top of the tower was a bronze figure of a Moorish horseman, fixed on a pivot, with his lance elevated upward. The horseman faced the city as though he were guarding it. If an enemy approached, the figure would turn in that direction and lower his lance as if preparing for action.

Aben Habuz was anxious to try out his new warning system. He didn't have to wait long. One morning he saw the face of the bronze horseman turn toward the mountains of Elvira and the lance point directly at the Pass of Lope. The king was ready to alert his army and place Granada on alert. The astrologer told him there was no need to do this and invited Aben Habuz to come with him to the secret hall in the tower.

As the king and the sage entered the hall, they saw that the window facing the Pass of Lope was open. The sage asked the king to look at the table in front of that window. The carved wooden cavalry and infantry were in motion. The astrologer observed that the king's enemies were already in the field advancing toward the Pass of Lope. Ibrahim told the king that, if he wanted to produce panic and confusion among them and cause them to retreat without loss of life, he must strike the wooden figures with the butt end of the magic lance on the table. If the king wanted to cause a bloody battle with carnage, he should strike the figures with the point of the lance.

Aben Habuz decided to draw a little blood. He thrust the magic lance point forward into some of the figures and touched other figures with the butt end of the lance. The astrologer had to restrain the king from completely eliminating his foe. He encouraged the king to send out scouts to the Pass of Lope. They returned with intelligence that a Christian army had advanced through the heart of the Sierra, almost within sight of Granada, when dissension had broken out among them. They had turned their weapons against each other and had retreated across the border after much slaughter.

Aben Habuz was overjoyed that the talisman had worked and that he now had all of his enemies within his power. He asked the sage what he wanted as a reward. Ibrahim claimed that the needs of an old man were simple. All he wanted was to outfit his cave so that he would be more comfortable. With the king's blessing, Ibrahim ordered additional rooms to be hewn out of solid rock and furnished with luxurious ottomans and divans. He hung the walls with the richest silks of Damascus and had baths constructed. He asked that the rooms be hung with many silver and crystal lamps. The royal treasurer groaned at the cost and complained to the king, in vain.

When the work had been completed, Ibrahim shut himself up in his new quarters for three days. Then he went to the treasurer and said that there was one more thing he required: dancing girls. He said that he only needed a few, but that they should be young and fair. The treasurer was surprised at the request, but he furnished them.

While Ibrahim lounged in his new quarters, the king carried on furious campaigns by remote control in the tower. He was delighted with the ease of his conquests. For a while he taunted his neighbors and tried to induce them to invade. Eventually they grew wary from repeated disasters until no one ventured to encroach on the king's territories. The king thought that things had become almost too quiet.

Finally one day, the talismanic horseman suddenly veered around, lowered his lance, and faced the mountains of Guadix. The magic table facing that direction was completely quiet, however. Perplexed, Aben Habuz sent a troop of cavalry to search the mountain and reconnoiter. The troop returned three days later without having sighted any enemy activity. They reported that all they found was a Christian damsel of unsurpassed beauty, whom they had captured as she was sleeping beside a fountain. The king asked to see the captive.

The young woman was arrayed with all the jewelry of Spanish women of that time. Pearls of dazzling whiteness were intertwined with her raven tresses, and the luster of her eyes rivaled the jewels that sparkled on her forehead. Around her neck was a golden chain suspending a silver lyre, which hung by her side. The king was totally captivated. The flashes of her dark eyes were like sparks of fire igniting the heart of Aben Habuz. The voluptuousness of her gait made his senses reel. The king asked her who she was and, furthermore, what she was.

The young woman told the king that she was the daughter of one of the Spanish princes, who until recently had ruled over this land. She said that the armies of her father had been destroyed, as if by magic, among these mountains. He had been driven into exile, and now she was a captive.

Ibrahim advised the king to be cautious. "Beware, oh king. This may be one of those northern sorceresses of whom we have heard, who assume the most seductive forms to beguile the unwary. I read witchcraft in her eye and sorcery in her every movement. Doubtless this is the enemy pointed out by the talisman."

The king replied, "Son of Abu Ayub, you are a wise man, but you are not as well versed in the ways of women as I am. As to this damsel, I see no harm in her; she is fair to look upon and finds favor in my eyes."

"Hear me, oh king!" replied the astrologer. "I have given you many victories by means of my talisman but have never shared in any of the spoils. Give me this stray captive to entertain me in my solitude with her silver lyre. If she is a sorceress, I have counter spells that could defy her charms."

The king reminded the sage of the three dancing girls and asked Ibrahim why he needed another woman. Ibrahim replied that he had three dancing girls but no singing women. He wanted to be serenaded when he was weary from studying.

The king refused; he insisted that he had marked this damsel for his own. Further pleadings from the astrologer accomplished nothing. After giving the king one more warning to be wary of this dangerous captive, the astrologer shut himself in his hermitage to brood over his disappointment. Aben Habuz resigned himself to his passion. His only goal now was to be looked upon favorably by the beauty.

The king did not have youth in his favor, but he had wealth and generosity. Aben Habuz devised all kinds of spectacles and entertainments for the object of his affection, including singing, dancing, tournaments, and bullfights. The princess received all of this splendor as due to her rank, or rather her beauty. She seemed to take pleasure in encouraging the monarch to incur expenses that shrunk his treasury. Then she treated his extravagant generosity as her right.

All this attention did not appear to make any impression on the heart of the princess. She never frowned at the king; but she never smiled at him either. Whenever the king professed his love, she began to play her silver lyre. Immediately the king nodded and became drowsy; gradually he fell asleep. He awoke refreshed, but with his ardor cooled for a time. All Granada scoffed at his infatuation.

Eventually Aben Habuz was confronted with a danger about which his talisman gave him no warning. An insurrection broke out in his capital; his palace was surrounded by an armed rabble, and his life and the life of the princess were at risk. He assembled his guards, dispersed the rebels, and crushed the insurrection. The king sought Ibrahim to acknowledge his warnings about the captive beauty and ask what he could do to avert similar perils. The sage told him to get rid of the damsel, who was the cause of his problems. The king answered that he would rather part with his kingdom.

The king asked the sage to devise some means of protecting him from the evils by which he was menaced. Aben Habuz wanted some quiet retreat where he could take refuge from the world and its cares and devote the remainder of his days to tranquillity and love. When the astrologer asked what his reward would be for providing such a retreat, the king invited Ibrahim to name his own reward.

Ibrahim asked whether the king had ever heard of the palace and garden of Irem in Arabia. Aben Habuz said that he had heard marvelous things about it from travelers but considered them wild fables. The sage replied that he had been there, and that the stories were true. Ibrahim promised that he could build a similar palace and garden on the mountain above the city using the secrets described in the book of knowledge of Solomon.

The king told the sage that he would give half his kingdom for such a retreat. Ibrahim said that he was old and easily satisfied; all he asked was for the contents of the first beast of burden that entered the gate of the new palace. The king agreed, and work was started on the palace on the summit of the hill, which would be topped by an impressive tower. When it was completed, Ibrahim came to the king and told him, "On the summit of the hill stands one of the most delectable palaces that ever the head of man devised or the heart of man desired. It contains sumptuous halls and galleries, delicious gardens, cool fountains, and fragrant baths. The entire mountain has been converted into a paradise. Like the garden of Irem, it is protected by a mighty charm, which hides it from the view of mortals, except those who possess the secret of the talisman."

The king was ready to take possession of his new palace the following morning. As soon as the rays of the sun shone on the snowy summit of the Sierra Nevada, the king mounted his steed and, accompanied by a few attendants, climbed the hill road to the new palace. Alongside him on a white palfrey rode the princess in her dress sparkling with jewels and with the silver lyre suspended around her neck. The astrologer walked on the other side of the king carrying a staff.

When they reached the summit, the king looked up but could see nothing. Ibrahim told him that the safeguard of the place was that nothing could be seen until the gateway had been passed. As they approached the gateway, the astrologer pointed out a mystic hand and key carved upon the arch. He told the king, "These are the talismans that guard the entrance to this paradise. Until that hand has reached down and seized the key, neither mortal power nor magic can provide access to the palace." While Aben Habuz was gazing at these talismans, the sage guided the palfrey of the princess through the gateway and into the courtyard.

At that, Ibrahim reminded Aben Habuz of his promised reward: the contents of the first beast of burden through the magic gateway. At first the king smiled, but when he realized that the sage was serious, he was indignant. He told the astrologer to take the strongest mule, load it with the most precious contents of the treasury, and take it, but not to consider taking the one who was the delight of the king's heart.

"What do I need of wealth?" cried the astrologer, scornfully. "I have the book of knowledge of Solomon and through it command the secret treasures of the world. The princess is mine by right. Your royal word is pledged. I claim her as my own."

The princess enjoyed this competition between the two graybeards; a light smile of scorn curled her lips. The wrath of the king got the better of his discretion. He told the astrologer that he might be the master of many arts but was not the king's master and not to presume to manipulate the king.

Ibrahim answered that the king couldn't claim superiority over someone who possessed the talismans of Solomon. The sage seized the bridle of the palfrey, struck the earth with his staff and sank with the princess through the center of the courtyard. The earth closed over them; no trace remained of the opening by which they had descended. Aben Habuz was astonished. He ordered a thousand workmen to dig into the ground where the astrologer had disappeared. They dug and dug in vain.

With the disappearance of Ibrahim, the benefits of the talismans ceased. The bronze horseman remained fixed, with his face turned toward the hill and his spear pointed to the place where the astrologer had disappeared, as though it was the location of the king's enemy. Occasionally the sound of music and a female voice could be heard coming from the center of the hill.

One day a peasant brought word to the king that during the night a fissure in the rock had opened up. When he looked in, the peasant saw a subterranean hall in which sat the astrologer on a magnificent divan, nodding off while listening the silver lyre of the princess. Aben Habuz looked for the fissure in the rock, but it had closed again. The summit of the mountain, the site of the promised palace and garden, remained a naked waste.

Aben Habuz's neighbors, finding him no longer protected by the magic spell, encroached on his territories from all sides. He contended with turmoil for the remainder of his life and eventually died without again enjoying peace.

The Alhambra was built on the mountain and reportedly approached the fabled delights of the palace of Irem. The spellbound gateway still exists and now forms the Gate of Justice, the grand entrance to the Alhambra. Under that gateway, it is said that the old astrologer remains in his subterranean hall, nodding on his divan and lulled by the silver lyre of the princess. The old invalid sentinels who guard the gate hear the strains occasionally on summer nights.

Ancient legends say that this will endure forever. The princess will remain a captive of the astrologer. The astrologer will continue to be led into magic slumber by the princess until the end of time, unless the mystic hand grasps the fated key and dispels the charm of this enchanted mountain.

Moral: Don't bite the hand that feeds you. Also, just because you have bested your adversaries doesn't mean that they will stay suppressed.

Based on: Washington Irving, "The Legend of the Arabian Astrologer," *The Alhambra*

The Legend of the Spirits' Mountain

On All Souls' Night I was awakened by the tolling of the bells. Their monotonous sound reminded me of a tale that I had heard in Soria, Spain. I tried to get to sleep again, but it was impossible. The imagination, once aroused, can be like a horse that runs wild and cannot be reined in. To pass the time, I decided to write the story down. I had heard it in the very place where it had occurred.

"Leash the dogs! Blow the horns to call the hunters together, and let us return to the city. Night is at hand—the night of All Souls, and we are on the Spirits' Mountain. Were it any day but this, I would not give up until I had made an end to that pack of wolves that the snows of Moncayo have driven from their dens; but today it is impossible. Very soon the Angelus will sound in the monastery of the Knights Templars, and the souls of the dead will begin to toll their bell in the chapel on the mountain."

"In that ruined chapel! Are you trying to frighten me?"

"No, I am not, fair cousin; but you are not aware of what happened here, for it is not yet a year since you came here from a distant part of Spain. Rein in your mare; I will keep mine at the same pace and tell you the story along the way."

The pages gathered in merry, boisterous groups; the Counts of Alcudiel and Borges mounted their noble steeds, and the entire company followed after Alonso and Beatriz, the son and daughter of those great houses, who rode in front of the company.

As they rode, Alonso related the promised story. "This mountain, which is now called the Spirits' Mountain, belonged to the Knights Templars, whose monastery you see over on the riverbank. The Templars were both monks and warriors. After Soria had been wrested from the Moors, the king summoned the Templars here from foreign lands to defend the city, thus offending his Castilian nobles, who, since they had won Soria by themselves, would have been able to defend it alone.

"Between the knights of the new and powerful order and the nobles of the city there existed for years an animosity that finally developed into a deadly hatred. The Templars claimed for their own this mountain, where they reserved an abundance of game to satisfy their needs. The nobles were determined to organize a great hunt on the mountain, despite the strong objections of the Templars, or "clergy with spurs," as they were called.

"The news of the proposed hunt spread fast, and nothing checked the nobles' determination to conduct the hunt and the Templars' resolve to prevent it. The great hunt was held, but the wild beasts did not remember it. Unfortunately, it was never forgotten by the mothers mourning their sons; it was not a hunting trip. It was a frightful battle. The mountain was strewn with corpses, and the wolves, whose extermination was the goal, had a bloody feast. Finally the mediation of the king was sought, and the mountain, the accursed cause of so many deaths, was declared abandoned. The chapel of the Templars on this same wild mountain, the site of friends and enemies buried together in its cloister, fell into ruins.

"They say that ever since, on All Souls' Night, the chapel bell is heard tolling all alone, and the spirits of the dead, wrapped in the tatters of their shrouds, run a fantastic chase through the bushes and brambles. The deer trumpet in terror, wolves howl, snakes hiss horribly, and the following morning the prints of the fleshless feet of skeletons are clearly marked in the snow. That is why it is called the Spirits' Mountain, and that is why I wanted to leave before nightfall."

Alonso finished his story just as the two young people arrived at the bridge to the city. They waited for the rest of the company to join them, and then the whole cavalcade moved together down the streets of Soria.

That evening after the servants had cleared the tables, the high Gothic fireplace of the palace of the Count of Alcudiel cast a vivid glow over the lords and ladies chatting in friendly fashion, gathered about the fire. The wind shook the leaded glass windows. Only two people were not participating in the general conversation: Beatriz and Alonso. Beatriz, absorbed in a vague reverie, followed the capricious dance of the flames with her eyes, and Alonso watched the reflection of the fire sparkling in the blue eyes of Beatriz. Neither of them spoke.

The duennas were telling gruesome stories, appropriate for the night of All Souls—stories in which ghosts and spectres played the principal roles. The church bells of Soria continued to toll mournfully in the distance.

"Fair cousin," finally exclaimed Alonso, breaking the long silence between them. "Soon we are to separate, perhaps forever. I know you do not like the arid plains of Castile, its rough soldier customs, and its simple patriarchal ways. Occasionally I have heard you sigh, perhaps for some lover in your faraway domain."

Beatriz made a gesture of cold indifference; the whole character of the young woman was revealed in that disdainful contraction of her delicate lips.

"Or perhaps for the grandeur and gaiety of the French capital, where you have also lived," the young man hastened to add. "In one way or another, I foresee that I shall lose you before long. When we part, I would like you to carry a remembrance of me. Do you recall the time we went to church to give thanks to God for restoring your health, which was your object in coming to this region? The jewel that fastened the plume of my cap attracted your attention. How well it would look clasping a veil over your dark hair! It has already been the adornment of a bride. My father gave it to my mother, and she wore it to the altar. Would you like it?"

"I do not know how it is in your part of the country," replied the beauty, "but in mine to accept a gift is to incur an obligation. Only on a holy day may one receive a present from a kinsman."

The frigid tone in which Beatriz spoke these words troubled the youth for a moment, but, clearing his brow of its wrinkles, he replied, "I know it, cousin, but today is the festival of All Saints, and yours among them—a holiday on which gifts are fitting. Will you accept mine?"

Beatriz slightly bit her lip and held out her hand for the jewel, without a word. The two fell silent once more and again heard the voices of the old women telling of witches and hobgoblins, the whistling wind that shook the windows, and the ongoing mournful, monotonous tolling of the bells. After a brief lapse of time, the conversation was resumed.

"Before All Saints' Day ends, which is holy to my saint as well as yours, can you, without compromising yourself, give me a keep-sake as well?" pleaded Alonso, looking into his cousin's eyes, which flashed like lightning and gleamed with a diabolical thought.

"Why not?" she exclaimed, raising her hand to her right shoulder as though seeking something in the folds of her velvet sleeve. Then, with an innocent air of disappointment, she said, "Do you remember the blue scarf that I wore today to the hunt, the scarf that you said, because of something about the meaning of its color, was the emblem of your soul?"

"Yes."

"Well, it is lost! It is lost, and I was thinking of letting you have it as a souvenir."

"Lost where?" asked Alonso, rising from his seat with an indescribable expression of mingled hope and fear.

"I do not know — perhaps on the mountain."

"On the Spirits' Mountain!" he murmured, paling and sinking back into his seat. "On the Spirits' Mountain!"

Then he went on in a voice choked and broken, "You know, for you have heard it a thousand times, that in the city I am called the king of the hunters. Not yet having had a chance to try, like my ancestors, my strength in battle, I have brought to this pastime, the image of war, all the energy of my youth, all the hereditary ardor of my race. On any other night I would fly for that scarf — fly as joyfully as to as festival; but tonight, this one night — why disguise it? — I am afraid. Do you hear? The bells are tolling, the Angelus has sounded in San Juan del Duero, and the ghosts of the mountain are now beginning to lift their yellowing skulls from amid the brambles that cover their graves — the ghosts! The mere sight of them is enough to curdle with horror the blood of the bravest, turn his hair white, or sweep him away in the stormy whirl of their fantastic chase."

While the young man was speaking, an almost imperceptible smile curled the lips of Beatriz. When he had finished speaking, she exclaimed in an indifferent tone, while stirring the fire on the hearth, where the wood blazed and snapped, throwing off sparks of a thousand colors, "Oh, by no means! What folly! To go to the mountain at this hour for such a trifle! On a dark night, too, with ghosts abroad, and the road endangered by wolves!"

As she spoke this closing phrase, she emphasized it with so

peculiar an intonation that Alonso could not fail to understand her bitter irony. As if moved by a spring, he jumped to his feet, passed his hand over his brow as if to dispel the fear in his brain, if not in his breast, and with a firm voice he addressed his beautiful cousin. "Farewell, Beatriz, farewell. If I return, it will be soon."

"Alonso, Alonso!" she called, turning quickly, but now that she had wished—or had made a show of wishing—to detain him, the youth had gone.

In a few moments she heard the beat of a horse's hoofs departing at a gallop. The beauty, with a radiant expression of satisfied pride flushing her cheeks, listened attentively to the sound that grew fainter and fainter until it died away. Meanwhile, the old dames continued their tales of ghostly apparitions; the wind made shrill noises against the balcony windows, and far away the bells of the city tolled on.

An hour passed, two, three. Midnight would soon be striking, and Beatriz withdrew to her chamber. Alonso had not returned, although less than an hour would have been enough for his errand.

"He must have been afraid!" exclaimed the girl. After a vain attempt to say some prayers for the dead for the coming Day of All Souls, she closed her prayer book and went to bed. She fell asleep; but her sleep was restless, light, and uneasy. The clock struck midnight. Beatriz heard through her dreams the slow, dull, melancholy strokes, and half opened her eyes. She thought that she had heard her name spoken, but far, far away, and in a faint, suffering voice. The wind groaned outside her window.

"It must have been the wind," she said, and, pressing her hand above her heart, she tried to calm herself. But her heart beat more wildly than ever. The doors to her chamber grated on their hinges with a long, loud creak. Then all the doors to her room flew open. She heard strange noises: the monotonous murmur of far-off water, the distant barking of dogs, confused voices, unintelligible words, echoes of footsteps coming and going, the rustle of garments, half-suppressed sighs, and labored breathing indicating the presence of something sensed but not seen in the darkness.

Beatriz, rigid with fear, thrust her head out from the bed curtains. She heard a thousand diverse voices and saw dim shapes moving around the room. She closed her eyes and tried to get back to sleep, but in vain. She got up again, paler, more terrified. This time she knew it was no illusion. She could hear slow footsteps on the carpet. The muffled footsteps were accompanied by the creaking sound of dry wood or bones. The footfalls came nearer and nearer; the prayer stool by the side of her bed moved.

The wind beat against the glass, the water of a far-off fountain fell with a monotonous, unceasing sound, the sound of barking dogs was carried by the wind, and the church bells of the city of Soria tolled sadly for the souls of the dead. The hour or two that passed like this seemed a century to Beatriz. Finally, day began to break. Putting aside her fear, she opened her eyes and welcomed the light of dawn.

Beatriz opened her bedcurtains, ready to laugh at her past alarms, when suddenly a cold sweat covered her body, her eyes seemed to be pulled out of their sockets, and a deadly pallor spread over her cheeks. On her prayer stool she had seen, torn and blood-stained, the blue scarf that she had lost on the mountain, the blue scarf that Alonso had sought.

Beatriz's attendants rushed in to tell her of the death of the heir of Alcudiel, whose body, partly eaten by wolves, had been found that morning among the brambles on the Spirits' Mountain. They found her motionless, clinging with both hands to one of the bedposts, her eyes staring, her mouth open, her lips white, her limbs rigid—dead, dead of fright!

Years later, a hunter, having lost his way, had to spend the Night of the Dead on the Spirits' Mountain. In the morning before he died, the hunter related what he had seen, a tale of horror. He said that he saw the skeletons of the ancient Knights Templars and of the nobles of Soria, buried in the chapel of the Templars, rise at the hour of the Angelus with a horrible rattle. They mounted their bony steeds and chased, as a wild beast, a beautiful woman, pallid, with streaming hair, who, uttering cries of terror and anguish, had been wandering, with bare and bloody feet, around the tomb of Alonso.

Moral: Goading someone to put pride ahead of reason can have
       unfortunate consequences.

Based on: Gustavo Adolfo Becquer, "The Spirits' Mountain,"
          Romantic Legends of Spain

The Cave of the Moor's Daughter

Opposite the Baths of Fitero, Spain, on a rocky, precipitous out-cropping at whose base flows the Alhama River, are the abandoned ruins of a Moorish castle celebrated in the glorious memories of the Reconquest of Spain as the location of great exploits, on the part of both the Moorish defenders and the attacking Spaniards. Only scattered ruins of the walls remain. The stones of the watchtower have fallen into the moat, and the coat of arms is covered with briars. In every direction, only broken arches and blackened, crumbling blocks of stone can be seen.

During my stay at the Baths, partly for exercise, which I was assured was good for my health, and partly from curiosity, I strolled every afternoon along the rough path that leads to the ruins of the Arab fortress. I passed many hours closely scanning the ground in hopes of discovering some fragments of armor and beating the walls to see if they were hollow and might be the hiding place of treasure. Also, I investigated all the nooks and crannies in an attempt to find an entrance to the underground cells that are thought to exist in all Moorish castles. Unfortunately, my searches were fruitless.

One afternoon when I had given up finding anything new and curious on the mountain crowned by the castle, I limited my walk to the banks of the river that flowed by its foot. As I walked along the riverbank, I saw a gaping hole in the rock, half hidden by thickly leafed bushes. Not without a little tremor, I parted the branches covering the entrance to what seemed a natural cave. After proceeding a few steps, I realized that it was a subterranean vault with a narrow mouth.

Because of the darkness I was not able to penetrate it to the end; however, I could see that the pathway went up some great stairs toward the castle, in whose ruins I recalled having seen a closed trapdoor. Apparently I had discovered one of those secret passages so common in fortifications of that time, serving as covert entrances and exits or for bringing in water from the river during a siege. I came out of the cave the same way I had entered and, to confirm what I had seen, I engaged a nearby workman in conversation.

We talked about many subjects: the medicinal properties of the waters of Fitero, the last harvest and the next, the women of

Navarre, and the cultivation of vines; in fact, we talked about virtually everything except the cave, which was the object of my curiosity. When our conversation got around to the cave, I asked the workman if he knew anybody who had gone through it and seen the other end.

"Gone through the Cave of the Moor's Daughter!" he repeated, astonished at hearing such a question. "Who would dare? Don't you know that a ghost comes out of this cave every night?"

"A ghost!" I exclaimed, stifling a smile. "Whose ghost?"

"The ghost of the daughter of a Moorish chief. She still wanders in mourning about these places and is seen every night coming out of this cave, dressed in white and filling a water jar at the river."

Through this good fellow I learned that there was a legend associated with this Arab castle and the vault connected to it. When the castle, which today is a shapeless ruin, was still held by the Moorish kings, the towers provided views of the beautiful valley kept fertile by the Alhama River. A hotly contested battle was fought in the valley near the town of Fitero. There a wounded Christian knight fell into the hands of the Arabs. He was taken to the fortress and placed in irons in the depths of a dungeon, where he struggled between life and death. Miraculously healed of his wounds, he was ransomed by the Spaniards.

The knight's men and brothers-in-arms were overjoyed to see him come home, supposing that he would call them to new combat; however, his soul had become possessed by a deep melancholy, and neither his relatives nor his friends could rid him of this strange gloom. During his imprisonment, he had seen the daughter of the Moorish chief. Word of her beauty had previously reached his ears. When he saw her, he found her so superior to his expectations that he could not resist the fascination of her charms. He fell desperately in love with one who could never be his bride.

The knight spent months devising daring, absurd plans to break the barriers that separated him from the young woman. Then he would try to forget her. The next day he would decide on another course of action. Finally, he summoned his men and his brothers-in-arms and made preparations to storm the fortress that sheltered the beautiful being who was the object of his love. Setting out on this expedition, everyone believed that their commander was motivated by eagerness to avenge his treatment in irons in the depths of the dungeon.

After the fortress was taken in a bloody battle, the true reason for that reckless enterprise, in which many good Christians had died, was hidden from no one. The knight, intoxicated with the love that he had succeeded in kindling in the breast of the beautiful Moorish girl, ignored the counsel of his friends and the murmuring of his soldiers. They recommended leaving the fortress as soon as possible, realizing that the Moors, recovered from the panic of their surprise attack, would counterattack soon.

The Moorish chief called together the Arabs from all around the region. One morning, the lookout in the watchtower announced that a cloud of warriors was descending from the mountain. It appeared that all of Mohammedanism was approaching to attack the castle. Hearing this, the Moor's daughter stood still, pale as death. The knight shouted orders to prepare to defend the castle. The portcullis was lowered, the drawbridge was raised, and the battlements were manned with archers.

The castle was impregnable; it could only be captured by surprise, as the Spaniards had taken it. Its defenders resisted many attacks. Finally, the Moors surrounded the castle and initiated a siege. Hunger began to ravage the Christians; however, knowing that the price of surrender would be the head of their leader, no one would betray him, not even those who had questioned his conduct earlier.

The Moors decided to make an assault in the middle of the night. The attack was furious; the defense, desperate; the encounter, horrible. The Moorish chief, his forehead shattered by a battle-ax, fell into the moat from the top of the battlements. Simultaneously the knight received a fatal blow fighting hand-to-hand in the tower. The Christians gave way and fell back.

The Moorish girl bent over her lover, who lay unconscious on the ground. She took him in her arms, and, with a strength increased by desperation, dragged him into the castle court. There she pressed a spring, causing a stone to move aside from the opening to a passageway. She disappeared with her precious burden and descended to the bottom of the vault.

When the knight recovered consciousness, he cried out, "I thirst! I die! I burn!" In his delirium, a precursor of death, the only words that passed his lips were those of agony, "I thirst! I burn! Water! Water! "

The Moorish girl knew that there was an opening from the valley through which the river flowed. Unfortunately, the valley and the mountains overlooking it were full of Moorish soldiers who, now that the fortress had surrendered, were looking everywhere for the knight and his beloved. Nevertheless, she did not hesitate for an instant; she took the helmet from the dying man, slipped like a shadow through the thicket covering the mouth of the cave, and went down to the river bank.

She had just filled the helmet with water and was returning to the side of her lover, when an arrow hissed and a cry was heard. Two Arab archers had aimed their bows in the direction from which they had heard the foliage rustle. The Moor's daughter, although mortally wounded, dragged herself to the entrance to the vault and down into its depths to join the knight.

The knight, seeing her bathed in blood and near death, recovered his reason and realized the enormity of his sin. He raised his eyes to heaven, took the water his beloved offered to him, and asked the Moorish girl, "Would you become a Christian? Would you die in my faith and, if I'm saved, be saved with me?" The young woman, who had fallen in a faint due to loss of blood, nodded. The knight poured the baptismal water over her, invoking the name of the Almighty.

The next day the soldier who had shot the arrow at the girl saw a trail of blood on the riverbank and followed it into the cave, where he found the bodies of the knight and his beloved. Ever since, the Moor's daughter has come out at night to wander around near the castle.

Moral: Exposing yourself to danger, possibly death, is your own decision. Exposing your comrades to a similar risk for personal reasons is beyond loyalty.

Based on: Gustavo Adolfo Becquer, "The Cave of the Moor's Daughter," *Romantic Legends of Spain*

Chapter 7

EMPATHETIC / COMPASSIONATE

By compassion we make others' misery our own,
and so, by relieving them, we relieve ourselves also.

Sir Thomas Browne, *Religio Medici*

The Lover of People

In India centuries ago lived a prince named Gautama. He lived in a splendid palace and was provided with every comfort. His father and mother wished that every day of his life would be one of perfect happiness. The prince grew up to be a tall, graceful young man who had never ventured beyond the beautiful gardens surrounding his father's palace.

The prince had never seen or heard of sorrow, sickness, or poverty. Everything evil or disagreeable had been kept out of his sight and hearing. He only knew of things that gave joy and good health and brought peace. When he became a man, he asked about the great world that existed outside the palace walls. He assumed that it was a beautiful, happy place. He wanted to learn all about it.

Gautama's parents agreed that it was a beautiful place, and that there were trees, flowers, rivers, and waterfalls, and many things to bring happiness. The prince decided to go out and see these things for himself. His parents begged him not to go. They reminded him of all the beautiful things that they had at the palace. They asked their son why he wanted to venture out where things were less beautiful. Nevertheless, they could see that his mind was set on going. They said no more.

The next morning, Gautama rode out from the palace in his carriage. He looked inquisitively at the houses on both sides of the street and at the faces of the children who stood in doorways as he passed. At first, he didn't see anything that bothered him. The word had gone out from the palace to remove anything that might be displeasing or painful.

The carriage turned into another street, one that had been less carefully prepared. No children appeared at the doors. Gautama saw a very old man, hobbling along a narrow section of the roadway. He asked who the man was, and why his face was pinched and his hair white. He also asked why the man's legs trembled under him, and why he was leaning on a stick. The prince observed that the old man's complexion was pale and that his eyes seemed weak. He wondered what kind of man this was.

The coachman told the prince that he was an old man who had lived more than eighty years, and that everyone who reached old age lost his or her strength and became feeble and gray. The prince asked if this were a condition that he would encounter. The coachman said that he would, if he lived long enough. Gautama asked what he meant by that, and did not everybody live eighty years? The coachman remained silent.

The coach passed into open country, where the prince saw the cottages of poor people. By the door of one of the cottages, a sick man was lying on a couch, pale and helpless. The prince asked why the man was lying there at that time of day. Gautama noticed that the man's face was white and that he seemed very weak. He asked if this man was old. The coachman replied that the man was sick, and that people are often sick. The prince asked why people get sick. The coachman explained it to the best of his ability.

Next, they saw a group of men working by the roadside. Their faces were browned by the sun; their hands were gnarled and dirty; their backs were bent from heavy lifting; their clothing was in tatters. The prince asked who the men were, what they were doing, and why they looked so downtrodden and unhappy. He was told that they were poor men working to improve the king's highway. He asked what poor men were. The coachman told him that most of the people in the world were poor and that they spent their time working for the rich. They had few joys and many sorrows.

Gautama exclaimed in amazement that this was not the beautiful, happy world that he had been told about. He realized how weak and foolish he had been to live in idleness and comfort when there was so much sadness and trouble all around him. The prince directed the coachman to return to the palace. He vowed never again to seek his own pleasure. He was determined to spend his life and to give all that he had to relieve the distress and sorrow that filled the world.

Prince Gautama kept his vow. One night he left the beautiful palace that his father had given to him and went out into the world to do good and to help his fellow man. To this day, millions of men remember and honor the name of Gautama as the great lover of humanity.

Moral: Giving is more noble than receiving. Helping the
       unfortunate brings its own reward.

Based on: James Baldwin, "The Lover of Men,"
          Fifty Famous People

Work, Death, and Sickness

A legend from the South American Indians relates a harsh story. According to this story, God at first made men so that they had no need to work. They needed neither houses, nor clothes, nor food, and everyone lived to be a hundred and did not know what illness was. After a while, God checked to see how people were doing. He saw that instead of being happy in their lives, they quarreled with one another and, each caring for himself, cursed life instead of enjoying it.

God realized that this was due to everyone living separately and looking out for himself or herself. God decided to change things by making it impossible to live without working. To avoid suffering and hunger, people would now have to build dwellings and cultivate the soil to grow grain and vegetables and to plant orchards. God thought that work would bring everyone together. He reasoned that, working as individuals, they could not make tools, cut and transport timber, build houses, sow and gather harvests, or spin and weave to make cloth and clothes.

God thought that this would make people understand that the more they worked together, the more they would have and the better they would live. He hoped that his would unite them. God gave it some time, and then came to see how men and women were living and whether or not they were happy. Unfortunately, He found them worse off than before. They had to work together to some extent, but not all together. They had broken up into small groups, and each group attempted to take work from other groups. They hindered one another, wasting time and effort, so that things did not go well with all of them.

God was disappointed that this change had not gone well. He decided to make another change: to arrange things so that men and women, instead of living a hundred years, would not know their time of death. God hoped that, realizing that they might die at any moment, people would be less likely to grasp short-term gains that would spoil the hours of life allotted to them. Nevertheless, it turned out otherwise. When God returned to see how people were living, He saw that their lives were worse than ever.

Those who were stronger subdued those who were weaker, killing some and threatening others. The strongest and their families did little work and suffered from their idleness. The weakest worked beyond their strength and suffered from lack of rest. Each group hated the other. People's lives had become even less happy.

Observing this, God decided to make another change. He spread all kinds of illnesses among them. God thought that if everyone were exposed to sickness, those who were well would help those who were sick, and when those who were well fell ill, they, in turn, would be cared for. Again, God went away. When He returned, He found that now that people were exposed to illnesses, their lives were worse than before. The sicknesses that God thought would unite men had divided them more than ever.

The strongest forced the weakest to wait on them, even when the weak were ill. The strongest did not come to the aid of others who were ill. The weak became so worn out that they could not look after their own sick and left them unattended. Because the sight of sick people might offend the wealthy, houses were established to accommodate the sick and the poor. They were attended by hired people who nursed them without compassion, occasionally with disgust. If an illness were infectious, those who were well avoided not only the sick but also those who attended them.

Finally, God said to Himself, "If even doing this will not bring men and women to understand where their happiness lies, let them be taught by suffering." Then God left men to themselves. Left alone, men lived a long time in misery before some of them realized that they could be and should be happy. In recent times, a few of them realized that work did not have to be a burden, but should be a common and happy occupation, uniting all men.

Men have begun to understand that with death constantly threatening them, the goal of every man should be to spend the years, months, hours, and minutes allotted him—in unity and love. They have begun to understand that illness, instead of dividing men, should provide the opportunity for loving one another.

Moral: In spite of all the suffering in the world, the time we are allotted in life should be spent in unity and love.

Based on: Leo Tolstoy, "Work, Death, and Sickness: A Legend," *Walk in the Light and Twenty-three Tales*

The Rich Brother and the Poor Brother

There once was a rich old farmer who had two sons. The younger son moved to the city to seek his fortune. After the old man's wife died, his elder son lived with him to look after the property. The young man got up very early in the morning and worked hard all day. At the end of every week, the father counted the money they had made and was delighted to see how large the pile of gold in the strongbox was becoming. He was so busy thinking about his money that he did not notice how bright his son's face had grown nor how he sometimes started when spoken to, as if his mind was far away.

One day the old man made one of his infrequent trips to the city on business. It was market day, and he met with many people that he knew. It was getting late when he went into the inn yard and asked to have his horse saddled. While he was waiting in the hall, the landlady came up to him. After a few remarks about the weather and the vineyards, she asked him how he liked his new daughter-in-law, and whether he was surprised at the marriage.

The old man gaped. He told her that he had no daughter-in-law and that he didn't know what she was talking about. That was exactly what the landlady, who was very curious, wanted to find out. She put on a look of great alarm and said that she hoped she hadn't caused any trouble. The old man observed that she had said much, but that she probably had more to say. So she told him, "It was not just for buying and selling that your handsome son came into town every week for months. He didn't take the shortest way, either. He rode over the river and across the hill past the cottage of Miguel the vinekeeper, whose daughter was the prettiest girl in the countryside. One morning they went to the little church on top of the hill and were married. My cousin is a servant to the priest, and she found out about it and told me. Good-day to you, sir; here is your horse. I must get back to work in the kitchen."

When the old man arrived home, he found his son. He told the young man that he knew everything, and that he was disappointed that his son had deceived him. He asked the young man to get out of his sight; he was done with him. The son tried to explain, but his father cut him off. His father told him that he was no son of his, and that he only had one son now. He ordered him to leave.

The young man turned away and walked heavily down a path to a cave in the side of the hill where he sat through the night, brooding. The son knew that he was in the wrong. He had meant to tell his father, and he was sure that his father would have forgiven his wife's poverty once he had seen her beauty and goodness. He had put off telling his father from day to day, always hoping for a better opportunity.

The son couldn't sleep that night, and neither could the father. The next morning the old man sent a messenger into the city to bring back his younger son. When the younger son arrived, his father told him that he was now the only heir, who would inherit all his lands and money. The father asked his younger son to come and live at home and to help him manage the property.

Although he was pleased to become a rich man—the brothers had never cared much for each other—the younger brother would rather have stayed in the city. However, he kept this to himself and worked hard as his brother had before him. The crops were not as good as they had been, and the father had to leave some fine houses he was building unfinished because it would take all of his savings to complete them. The old man would never allow the name of his older son to be mentioned, and he never saw him again. When he died, he left all his lands and money to the younger son.

Meanwhile the disinherited son had grown poorer and poorer. He and his wife were always looking for work. They were frugal, but luck was against them. At the time of his father's death, they had neither enough food to eat nor enough clothes to wear. The older son couldn't bear to see his children grow weaker and weaker every day. At last, swallowing his pride, he walked across the mountains to his old home, where his brother lived.

It was the first time in years that the brothers had seen each other. They looked each other over in silence. Finally, the older brother blinked away some tears and asked, "Brother, I don't have to tell you how poor I am; you can see that for yourself. I have not come to beg for money, but only to ask if you would give me those unfinished houses of yours in the city. I will make them watertight, so that my wife and children can live in them; that will save our rent. As they are, they profit you nothing."

The younger brother listened and pitied his brother. He gave him the houses that he had asked for, and the older brother went away happy. Years went by and the younger brother was lonely. He decided that it was time that he married. The wife that he chose was wealthy, but she was also greedy. No matter how much she had, she always wanted more. Unfortunately, she was one of those people who thought that the possessions of other people were better than her own. Frequently her husband regretted the day that he had met her; her meanness and shabby ways put him to shame. He could not control her, and she got worse and worse.

After several months of marriage, the new bride went into the city to buy some dresses. When she had finished shopping, she decided to visit her unknown sister-in-law. Her in-laws' house was on a broad street and should have been magnificent, but the carved stone portico enclosed a mean little door of rough wood. A row of beautiful pillars led to nothing. The dwellings on each side were in the same unfinished condition, and water trickled down the walls. However, the greedy bride saw that by spending some money on the houses, she could make them as splendid as originally intended. She decided to get them for herself.

The new bride walked up the marble staircase and entered the little room where her sister-in-law sat, making clothes for her children. The younger brother's wife expressed an interest in the houses and asked many questions about them. Her new relations liked her more than they thought they would and hoped that they might become good friends.

However, as soon as the younger brother's wife returned home, she told her husband that he must get those houses back from his brother. She claimed that they would exactly suit her, and that she could easily make them into fine homes. He responded that she could buy houses in another part of the city, but that she couldn't have those. He reminded her that he had long ago given those to his brother, who had lived in them for many years.

The older brother's wife grew very angry and began to cry so loudly that all of the neighbors were aroused. She argued that giving away those houses was absurd and unjust; furthermore, he had done it when he was still a bachelor and now things had changed. Finally, her exasperated husband agreed to summon his brother to a court of law where he would say that the houses had only been loaned.

When all the evidence had been heard, the judge ruled in favor of the poor man. This made the rich wife even more angry, so she appealed the verdict in several higher courts. Eventually, a final appeal was scheduled to be heard by the highest court in the city.

The brothers set out on their journey to the city, one on horseback and the other on foot. The rich one had plenty of food in his knapsack; the poor one had nothing but a piece of bread and several onions. At dusk, they were both glad to see lights near a farmhouse in the distance.

The lights had been placed there by the farmer, who had prepared a fine supper to celebrate his wife's birthday. He invited the rich brother to come in and sit down; he hesitated but eventually also invited the poor brother. Supper was served and the younger brother ate heartily, famished from the long trip. The farmer's wife would touch nothing. She said that the only supper she wanted was one of the onions that the poor man was cooking at the fire. He gave her an onion, and soon they all went to bed. The poor man curled up in the corner on the floor.

A few hours later, the farmer was awakened by the cries and groans of his wife. She told him that she felt so ill that she thought she was going to die. She blamed it on the onion that she had eaten and said that it must have been poisoned. The farmer exclaimed that the older brother would pay for this, and grabbed a thick stick and began to beat the poor man, even though he had been sound asleep and had nothing with which to defend himself. Fortunately the noise aroused the younger brother who snatched the stick from the farmer's hand and told him, "We are going into the city to try a lawsuit. Come along with us and accuse him if you think that he attempted to poison your wife. Don't kill him now; you will only get yourself in trouble."

The farmer acknowledged that the rich brother was probably right and agreed to go into the city with them to ensure that the poor man got what was coming to him. It had rained heavily, and the road had become so muddy that it was virtually impassable. A mule laden with baggage was stuck in the mud, and the master had been unable to pull it out. He appealed to the younger brother and the farmer, who were on horseback, but they ignored his pleas.

Soon the poor brother, spattered with mud from head to foot from walking along the road, stopped and offered to help the muleteer. The poor brother grabbed the mule's tail and pulled, hauling the burdened mule to dry ground, but at the expense of pulling off the mule's tail. The muleteer was furious, forgetting that, without the help he had received, he would probably have lost the mule altogether. He yelled at the poor man, declaring that he had ruined his beast, and that the law would make him pay for it.

The ungrateful muleteer jumped on the back of the mule, which was so glad to be out of the mud that it did not seem to mind the loss of its tail. By evening the muleteer reached the inn in the city, where the rich man and the farmer had already arrived for the night. Meanwhile the poor brother walked wearily along, wondering what other dreadful adventures were in store for him. He thought that he certainly would be condemned for one of the accusations, and that if he had to lose his life, he would rather choose the manner of his own death than let his enemies decide.

As soon as the poor brother entered the city, he looked around for a suitable place to carry out his plan. When he found the place he was looking for, it was too dark for him to be sure of success. He curled up in a doorway and slept until morning. He awoke thinking that this was the last day of his life. Although he regretted leaving his wife and children behind him, he had struggled so long that he was very tired. He would have liked to have proven his innocence, but everyone had been too clever for him. He climbed the stone steps that led to the battlements of the city and looked around.

A sick old man who lived nearby had asked to be laid at the foot of the wall so that the beams of the rising sun might fall upon him. Little did he realize that directly above him on the top of the battlements, exactly over his head, stood a man taking a last look at the sun before jumping to his death. The poor brother closed his eyes and leaped forward. The wall was high, and he fell rapidly; however, it wasn't the ground that he fell on but the body of the sick man, who died with a groan.

As he stood up unhurt, the arms of the poor brother were seized and held by two young men who informed him that he had killed their father. They told him that they were taking him before the judge to answer for it. The poor brother told them that he didn't know their father and asked what they were talking about. He could not think of why he should be accused of this fresh crime, but he received no answers to his questions.

The poor brother was hurried through the streets to the court-house, where his brother, the farmer, and the muleteer had just arrived, all angry as ever and talking at once, until the judge entered and called for silence. The judge told them that he would hear them one at a time and motioned for the younger brother to begin. The younger brother stated that the unfinished houses were his, left to him with the rest of the estate by his father, and that his brother refused to give them up.

The poor brother explained how he had begged the houses from his brother, and he produced the gift deeds that made him their owner. The judge listened quietly, asked a few questions, and pronounced his verdict that the houses would reman the property of the poor brother to whom they had been given. Furthermore, he told the younger brother that he had brought this accusation knowing that it was wicked and unjust. He ordered the rich brother, in addition to losing the houses, to pay damages of a thousand pounds to his brother.

Next the farmer told his tale. The judge could hardly conceal a smile at the story. He asked the farmer whether his wife was dead before he left the house. The farmer had to admit that he had been in such a hurry for justice to be done that he had not waited to see. The poor brother then testified, and once more judgement was in his favor, with damages of twelve hundred pounds awarded to him.

The muleteer was informed very plainly that he had been mean and ungrateful for the help that had been given to him; as punishment, he was ordered to pay the poor man fifty pounds and to let him have the use of the mule until its tail had grown back again.

Finally, the two sons of the sick man told the judge that this was the wretch who had killed their father, and they demanded that he should die also. The judge asked the poor man how he had killed the sick man. The poor brother recounted how he had jumped from the wall, not knowing that anyone had been beneath him.

"This is my judgement," announced the judge, "Let the accused sit under the wall, and let the sons of the dead man jump from the top and fall on him and kill him; if they will not do this, they are obligated to pay eight hundred pounds for their false accusation."

The young men looked at each other and slowly shook their heads. They told the judge that they would pay the fine, and the judge nodded. The poor man rode the mule home and brought enough money back to his family to keep them in comfort for the rest of their lives.

Moral: Sometimes when everything is going against us, we have
only to hang on until the tide turns in our favor.

Based on: Andrew Lang, "The Rich Brother and Poor Brother,"
The Lilac Fairy Book

The House in the Wood

A poor woodcutter lived with his wife and three daughters in a little hut on the edge of a great forest. One morning as the woodcutter was going to work, he told his wife to have the eldest daughter
bring his lunch to him in the woods. He said he would take a bag
of millet with him to sprinkle on the path so she would not get lost.

When the sun was high over the forest, the girl set out with a
basin of soup. Unfortunately, the sparrows, larks, finches, and
blackbirds had picked up the millet long before, and the girl could
not find her way.

Completely lost, the girl walked on and on until the sun had set.
The trees rustled in the darkness, the owls hooted, and she was
frightened. Finally she saw a twinkling light in the distance among
the trees. Hoping that the people living there would take her in for
the night, she walked toward the light.

When she reached the house, she knocked on the door and a
gruff voice told her to come in. She walked in an saw an old, gray-
haired man sitting at the table. His face rested on his hands, and his
beard flowed over the table almost to the ground. A hen, a cock, and
a cow lay near the stove. The girl told the man her story and asked
for a night's lodging. The man said:

> Pretty cock,
> Pretty hen,
> And you, pretty cow,
> What do you say?

In response, the animals made noises that were interpreted by
the old man as agreeing to let her stay there. The old man told her
that they had an abundance of food and she could go into the
kitchen and cook them supper. The girl found plenty of everything
in the kitchen and cooked a meal, but she didn't think of the ani-

mals. She placed the food on the table, sat down opposite the gray-haired man, and ate until she was full. After the meal, the girl said that she was tired and asked if there was a bed in which she could sleep. The animals answered:

> You have eaten with him,
> You have drunk with him,
> Of us you have not thought,
> Sleep then as you ought.

The old man told the girl to go upstairs to the bedroom, make the bed with clean sheets, and go to sleep. She went upstairs, made the bed, and lay down. After a while the old man looked in on her by the light of a candle and shook his head. When he saw that she was asleep, he opened a trapdoor and let her fall into the cellar.

When the woodcutter came home late in the evening, he scolded his wife for leaving him all day without food. She replied that she had sent the oldest daughter to take him food. They agreed that she must have lost her way but would return home the next day.

At daybreak the woodcutter asked his second-oldest daughter to bring his food to him, and he set off into the woods. This time he took a bag of lentils to mark the path. He reasoned that lentils were larger than millet and that the girl would see them better and be able to find her way. At midday the girl went into the woods with the food for her father, but the birds of the woods had eaten all of the lentils. She wandered around in the forest until nightfall, when she came to the house in the woods. As her sister had, she asked for food and a night's lodging. The old man with the gray hair again asked the animals:

> Pretty cock,
> Pretty hen,
> And you, pretty cow,
> What do you say?

The animals answered as before and everything happened as on the previous day. The girl cooked a good meal, ate and drank with the old man, and did not trouble herself about the animals. When she asked for a bed for the night, the animals answered:

You have eaten with him,
You have drunk with him,
Of us you have not thought,
Now sleep as you ought.

When she was asleep, the old man shook his head over her and let her fall into the cellar.

On the third morning the woodcutter asked his wife to send the youngest daughter with his meal. He observed that she was always good and obedient and would keep to the right path and not wander off like her sisters.

When his wife expressed concern about losing her dearest child, the woodcutter told her not to worry because the youngest was too clever to lose her way. Furthermore, he added that he would drop peas along the path. Since they were larger than lentils, they would show her the way.

At midday, the youngest daughter went into the woods with a basket of food on her arm. Unfortunately, the pigeons had eaten the peas, and she did not know which way to go. She was distressed as she thought of her hungry father and her worried mother. At last, after night fell, she saw the light in the distance and came to the house in the woods. She asked the old man if she could stay for the night, and again he asked the animals:

Pretty cock,
Pretty hen,
And you, pretty cow,
What do you say?

The animals responded as before. The young girl walked over to the stove where the animals were lying and stroked the cock and the hen and scratched the cow on the head. As requested by the old man, she prepared a good supper and placed the food on the table. Then she asked, "Shall I have plenty while the good animals have nothing? There is food to spare outside; I will attend to them first." She went outside to get barley that she spread near the cock and the hen. She brought the cow an armful of sweet-smelling hay. After inviting them to eat their food, she filled a bowl of water for them.

When the animals were satisfied, the young girl sat down beside the old man and ate what was left for her. Soon the cock and the hen tucked their heads under their wings and the cow blinked its eyes, so the maiden said, "Shall we go to rest now?" The animals said:

> You have eaten with us,
> You have drunk with us,
> You have tended us right,
> So we wish you good night.

The maiden went upstairs, made the bed with clean sheets, and fell asleep. She slept peacefully until midnight when there was such a loud noise in the house that she woke up. Everything trembled and shook; the animals sprang up and dashed themselves against the wall; the beams swayed as though they would be torn from their foundations. The stairs came tumbling down, and the roof fell in with a crash. Then all became still. Since no harm had come to the maiden, she lay down and went back to sleep.

When the youngest daughter awoke in broad daylight, an amazing sight met her eyes. She was in a room furnished with royal splendor. The walls were covered with golden flowers on a green background; the bed was made of ivory and the bedspread of velvet. On a stool near her were a pair of slippers studded with pearls. The maiden thought that she must be dreaming until three richly dressed servants entered the chamber and asked what her commands were.

She told them she would get up at once and cook the old man's breakfast for him and then feed the pretty cock, hen, and cow.

At those words, the door opened and a handsome young man entered. He explained that he was a king's son who had been condemned by a wicked witch to live as an old man in the woods with no company other than his three servants, who had been transformed into a cock, a hen, and a cow. He told her that the spell could only be broken by the arrival of a maiden who would show herself to be kind not only to men but also to beasts. He told her that she was that maiden and that last night at midnight they were freed. The humble house in the woods had been transformed into his royal palace.

The prince proposed to the maiden, and she accepted. The prince told his servant to bring the maiden's parents to the palace so that they could be present at the wedding feast.

The maiden asked what had happened to her two sisters. The prince told her that they had been shut up in the cellar, but that they would be led into the forest to work for a charcoal burner until they had learned to be more compassionate and never again to let poor animals go hungry.

Moral: Things aren't always what they appear to be.
      Compassion should be shown to all living creatures.

Based on: Andrew Lang, "The House in the Wood,"
The Pink Fairy Book

The Piece of String

Along all the roads around Goderville, France, peasants and their wives were coming to town for market day. The men walked with slow steps, their bodies bent forward on legs deformed by the hard work of reaping wheat. Some led a cow or calf by a cord. The wives walked behind, spurring the animals on when required and carrying baskets of chickens and ducks. The women walked with a livelier step than their husbands did. The public square of Goderville was crowded with people and animals. The clamoring voices and animal sounds made a continuous din.

Monsieur Hauchecome of Breaute had just arrived in Goderville and was walking toward the public square when he saw a small piece of string on the ground. Hauchecome, economical like all natives of Normandy, thought that everything useful should be kept. He bent over and took the bit of thin cord from the ground and was rolling it up carefully when he noticed Monsieur Malandain, the harness-maker, standing in his doorway looking at him.

They had previous business together about a halter, and they were not on good terms. Both knew how to hate. Hauchecome was embarrassed to be seen picking a piece of string out of the dirt. He quickly concealed the string in his pocket and pretended to be looking for something on the ground that he could not find. Then he walked toward the market.

Hauchecome was soon lost in the flow of the crowd, which was busy with bargaining. By noontime the square was deserted. Everyone had left for lunch. The courtyard outside of Jourdain's was filled with vehicles of all kinds, including carts, gigs, and wagons. The great room of the restaurant was filled with people, and three spits were turning with appetizing food. All the farm aristocracy ate at Jourdain's and talked about the weather and their day-to-day activities.

Suddenly a drum beat in the courtyard, and everyone ran to the door and windows to hear the announcement of the public crier: "It is hereby made known to the inhabitants of Goderville, and in general to all persons present at the market, that there was lost this morning on the road to Benzeville, between nine and ten o'clock, a black leather pocketbook containing five hundred francs and some business papers. The finder is requested to return same with all haste to the mayor's office or to Monsieur Fortune Houlbreque of Manneville. A reward of twenty francs is offered."

The crier went on his way, and everyone began to speculate about what chance Houlbreque had of finding his pocketbook. As the diners were finishing their meals, the chief of gendarmes appeared in the doorway and asked if Monsieur Hauchecome of Breaute was there. Hauchecome identified himself and was asked to accompany the chief of gendarmes to the mayor's office.

The mayor, a pompous man, was waiting to talk with him. He said, "Monsieur Hauchecome, you were seen this morning picking up, on the road to Benzeville, the pocketbook lost by Houlbreque of Manneville." The astounded peasant looked at the mayor and denied it. He was told that he had been seen picking it up. When he asked by whom, he was told by Monsieur Malandain, the harness-maker. The old man understood what was going on and flushed with anger. He replied that the harness-maker had seen him pick up a piece of string, and he took it out of his pocket to show him.

The mayor, incredulous, shook his head and asked Hauchecome if he expected him to believe that Malandain, a man of his word, mistook the cord for a pocketbook. The peasant said, nevertheless, that this was the truth and that he would stake the salvation of his soul on it. The mayor then said that after picking up the pocketbook, Hauchecome had been seen looking in the mud to see if any money had fallen out of it.

The old man, choked with indignation, asked how anyone could tell such lies to take away an honest man's reputation. There was no use protesting. No one believed him. He was confronted by Malandain, who repeated and maintained his accusation. They shouted at each other for an hour. At his own request, Hauchecome was searched. Nothing was found on him. Finally the mayor discharged him and told him that he would consult the public prosecutor for further instructions.

The news had spread. As Hauchecome left the mayor's office, he was confronted by questioners. He told them the story of the string, but no one believed him. They laughed at him. He became exasperated, repeated himself, and was distressed that nobody believed his story. He stopped in the village of Breaute to explain it to everyone. They didn't believe him either. By the time he went to bed, he was ill.

The next day at about one o'clock in the afternoon, Marius Paumelle, a hired man in the employ of Monsieur Breton, husbandman at Ymanville, returned the pocketbook and its contents to Houlbreque of Manneville. He claimed to have found the pocketbook in the road and, not knowing how to read, had carried it to his employer.

The news spread. Hauchecome immediately went to talk with the people he had seen the previous day and recounted his story but with a happy ending. He was triumphant. He told them that what had bothered him the most was not the thing itself, but the lying. He told them that there was nothing more shameful than being placed under a cloud because of a lie.

Hauchecome talked about his adventure all day, even to strangers. He was calm now, but something was bothering him that he couldn't define. People had a look of humor about them when he talked to them. They did not seem convinced. He perceived that they were talking about him behind his back. The following week when he went to Goderville, Malandain laughed at him as he walked by. Hauchecome didn't know why a farmer from Crequetot called him a big rascal.

A horse dealer from Monvilliers told him that he had heard about the piece of string, called him a sharper, and told him that he knew about that old trick. Hauchecome stammered that the pocketbook had been found. The horse dealer said that there was one that finds and one that reports. In any case, he was sure that Hauchecome was mixed up in it. Now Hauchecome understood; they were accusing him of having had the pocketbook returned by an accomplice.

When Hauchecome protested at Jourdain's, the entire table began to laugh. He couldn't finish his dinner. He left the restaurant to a chorus of jeers. He went home, ashamed and indignant, choking with anger. He was stricken to the heart with the injustice of the suspicion. He recounted his adventure to himself of his waking hours. Behind his back, they said that all of his excuses were lies. He sensed it and was consumed by it. He wasted away before their eyes.

The wags now made Hauchecome tell about the string to amuse them, just as they made an old soldier who had been on a campaign tell about his battles. Hauchecome's mind, touched deeply, began to weaken. He took to his bed toward the end of December. He died in early January. In the delirium of his death struggle he continued to claim his innocence, reiterating, "A piece of string, a piece of string—look—here it is, Monsieur Mayor."

* * *

The Three Gates

If you are tempted to reveal
A tale to you someone has told
About another, make it pass,
Before you speak, three gates of gold.
These narrow gates: First, "Is it true?"
Then, "Is it needful?" In your mind
Give a truthful answer. And the next
Is last and narrowest, "Is it kind?"
And if to reach your lips at last
It passes through these gateways three,
Then you may tell the tale, nor fear
What the result of speech may be.

From *The Arabian*

Moral: Once a reputation is lost, it is impossible to restore it completely.

Based on: Guy de Maupassant, "The Piece of String," *The Best Stories of Guy de Maupassant*

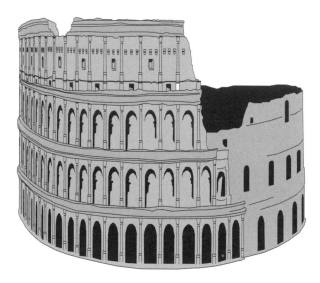

Chapter 8

SPECIAL / MEMORABLE

SUCCESS

I hold no dream of fortune vast,
Nor seek undying fame.
I do not ask when life is past
That many know my name.
I may not own the skill to rise
To glory's topmost height,
Nor win a place among the wise,
But I can keep the right.
And I can live my life on earth
Contented to the end,
If but a few shall know my worth
And proudly call me friend.

Edgar A. Guest

The Open French Doors

Framton Nuttel was advised to leave the city and spend some quiet time in the country to relax his nerves. Unfortunately, he didn't know anyone in the small village where he would be staying. His sister had visited the village and offered to give him letters of introduction to people she knew there. She said, "Some of them, as far as I remember, were quite nice." She added, as he was preparing to visit his rural retreat, "I know how it will be. You will bury yourself down there and not speak to living soul, and your nerves will be worse than ever from moping."

Framton's first opportunity to present a letter of introduction was at the home of Mrs. Sappleton. He hoped that she was one of the "nice" people. He was greeted by Mrs. Sappleton's niece, a self-possessed young lady of fifteen. She told Framton that her aunt would be down shortly and that in the meantime, he must put up with her. He attempted to say something that would flatter her while waiting for the aunt. He doubted more than ever whether these formal visits with total strangers would do much to help the nerve cure that he was supposed to be undertaking.

After a period of silence, the niece asked Framton whether he knew many people in the village. He admitted that he knew hardly anybody, and that his sister had stayed in the village four years ago and had given him letters of introduction to some of the residents. The young woman said, "Then you know practically nothing about my aunt?"

He admitted that he knew only her name and address. He wondered if she were married or a widow.

The young woman confided, "Her great tragedy happened just three years ago. That would be since your sister's time." Framton asked, "Her tragedy?" Somehow tragedies seemed out of place in this restful country spot. The niece pointed to a pair of French doors that opened onto the lawn, and said, "You may wonder why we keep those doors open on an October afternoon."

Framton noted that it was quite warm for that time of year and inquired if the open doors had anything to do with the tragedy.

The young woman said, "Out through those doors, three years ago to the day, her husband and her two young brothers went off for their day's shooting. They never came back. In crossing the moor to their favorite snipe-shooting ground, they were all engulfed in a

139

treacherous bog. It had been a dreadfully wet summer and places that were safe in other years gave way suddenly without warning. Their bodies were never recovered. That was the worst part of it."

Here the young woman's voice lost its self-possessed tone and became falteringly human. "Poor aunt always thinks that they will come back someday, they and the little brown spaniel that was lost with them, and walk through those doors as they used to. That is why the doors are left open every evening until dusk. Poor, dear aunt, she had often told me how they went out, her husband with his white raincoat over his arm, and Ronnie, her youngest brother, singing, 'Bertie, why do you bound?' as he always did to tease her, because he said it got on her nerves. Do you know, sometimes on still, quiet evenings like this, I almost get a creepy feeling that they will walk in through those doors." The young woman broke off with a shudder.

Framton was relieved when the aunt walked briskly into the room with many apologies for being late.

She said, "I hope that Vera has been amusing you?" Framton admitted that she had been very interesting.

Mrs. Sappleton said, "I hope you don't mind the open French doors. My husband and brothers will be home directly from shooting, and they always come in that way. They've been out hunting for snipe in the marshes today, so they'll make a fine mess on my poor carpets when they come in."

Mrs. Sappleton rattled on cheerfully about the shooting and the scarcity of birds, as well as the prospect for ducks during the winter. Framton was horrified. He attempted to change the subject without success. He could see that his hostess was giving him only divided attention. She kept looking beyond him to the open doors and the lawn beyond. He thought how unfortunate it was that his visit was on the third anniversary of the tragedy.

Framton told Mrs. Sappleton that his doctors had prescribed complete rest for him, an absence of mental excitement, and the avoidance of violent physical exercise. He added that it wasn't as clear concerning diet restrictions that he should consider. He assumed that Mrs. Sappleton, a complete stranger, was interested in his health problem. She suppressed a yawn.

Finally, Mrs.Sappleton cried out, "Here they are at last! Just in time for tea, looking very muddy." Framton turned toward the niece with a look intended to convey sympathetic comprehension. The young woman was staring at the lawn beyond the doors with dazed horror in her eyes. Fearfully, Framton turned around in his chair and looked in the same direction.

In the twilight, three figures were walking across the lawn toward the French doors. They all carried guns under their arms, and one of them had a white coat hung over his shoulders. A tired brown spaniel kept close to their heels. As they approached the house, a young voice rang out, "Bertie, why do you bound?"

Framton grabbed wildly for his hat and ran through the hall doorway, down the gravel driveway, and through the front gate. A young man on a bicycle had to steer into a hedge to avoid colliding with him.

Mr. Sappleton asked who had bolted as they came into the room. His wife said, "A most extraordinary man, a Mr. Nuttel, who could only talk about his illness, and dashed off without a word of goodbye or apology when you arrived. One would think he had seen a ghost." The niece calmly added, "I expect it was the spaniel. He told me that he had a horror of dogs. He was once hunted into a cemetery on the banks of the Ganges River by a pack of dogs, and had to spend the night in a newly dug grave with the dogs snarling and foaming just above him. Enough to make anyone lose their nerve."

Moral: Look beyond the words. Things aren't always what they appear to be.

Based on: H. H. Monro, "The Open Window," *The Short Stories of Saki*

For Want of a Horseshoe Nail

In 1485, Henry Tudor, the Earl of Richmond, returned from exile in France to reclaim the Lancastrian right to the throne of England from King Richard III. On the road to Market Bosworth, he met the Stanley brothers, both of whom had strong military forces in the area. Lord Stanley was Tudor's stepfather, and Sir William Stanley was already considered a traitor by King Richard and his Yorkists.

Richard III, a better soldier than his challenger, placed the

Duke of Norfolk in charge of his vanguard; the Earl of Northumberland commanded the rear of the king's army. The crisis of the Battle of Bosworth Field came when the Stanleys moved against the Yorkist flanks and Northumberland failed to intervene. The outnumbered Yorkist army melted away and wasn't pursued by Tudor. Richard, preferring death to capture, was unhorsed and killed. Richard's defeat was immortalized by Shakespeare's famous line: "A horse! A horse! My kingdom for a horse!"

The morning of the battle, Richard had sent a groom to ensure that his favorite horse was ready for the coming battle. The groom told the blacksmith to shoe the horse quickly, because the king wanted to ride at the head of his troops. The blacksmith told the groom that he would have to wait because he had shod the king's entire army over the last few days, and he was out of iron.

The groom told the blacksmith that he couldn't wait since the Lancastrian army was already advancing, and they must be met on the field. The blacksmith was told to make do with what he had. The blacksmith made four horseshoes from a bar of iron. He hammered, shaped, and fitted them to the horse's hoofs. He began to nail them on but after fastening two shoes on, he found that he didn't have enough nails for the other two. He told the groom that he had only six nails, and that it would take time to hammer out ten more.

The groom said that he couldn't wait. He could hear the trumpets sounding the advance. He asked the blacksmith to use what he had, to put three nails each on the remaining two shoes. The blacksmith said he could put the shoes on, but they wouldn't be as secure as the others. The groom asked if they would hold, and the blacksmith admitted that he couldn't be certain. The groom told him just to nail them on and to hurry.

The armies clashed, and Richard was in the thick of the battle. He rode up and down the line fighting and urging his troops onward. On the other side of the field, he saw some of his men falling back. If others saw them, it might signal a retreat. So Richard spurred his horse and galloped toward the broken line, calling on his men to turn and fight.

Richard was only halfway across the field when one of his horse's shoes flew off. The horse stumbled and fell, and the king was thrown from his horse. Before Richard could grab the reins, the terrified animal got up and galloped away. Richard looked around and saw that his soldiers also were turning and running, and that Tudor's troops were closing in.

Richard waved his sword in the air and shouted, "A horse! A horse! My kingdom for a horse!" But there was no horse available to him. His army had broken and run, and his men were just trying to save themselves. A moment later Tudor's soldiers were upon Richard, and the battle was over.

A nursery rhyme has come down from that time:

> For want of a nail, a shoe was lost,
> For want of a shoe, a horse was lost,
> For want of a horse, a battle was lost,
> For want of a battle, a kingdom was lost,
> And all for the want of a horseshoe nail.

Moral: Take care of little problems before they become
      big problems.

Based on: James Baldwin, "The Horseshoe Nails,"
      Fifty Famous People

The Lady, or the Tiger

Years ago, there lived a semi-barbaric king whose ideas, although somewhat polished by cultured neighbors, were ambitious and untrammeled, as would be expected from the half of him that was barbaric. He was exuberant and unrestricted. If he wanted to do something, he did it. When everything was going his way, he was genial. When there was a hitch, he was more genial still while he eliminated the cause of the problem.

One example of his barbarism was the public arena, where, in his opinion, the minds of his subjects could be refined by exhibitions of manly and beastly valor. The arena was built, not to allow the people to hear dying gladiators, nor to enable them to view the conflict between religious opinions and hungry jaws, but to develop the mental energies of the people. The king viewed the vast amphitheater, with its encircling galleries and its unseen vaults and passages, as an agent of poetic justice, in which crime was punished, or virtue rewarded, by decrees of impartial chance.

When a subject was accused of a crime of sufficient importance to interest the king, public notice was given that on an appointed day the person's fate would be decided in the king's arena. When the people were assembled in the galleries, and the king, surrounded by his court, gave a signal from high up on his throne on one side of the arena, the door beneath him opened and the accused subject stepped out into the amphitheater. Directly opposite him, on the other side of the arena, were two doors, side by side and exactly alike.

It was the duty of the accused subject to walk to these doors and open one of them. He was not influenced in any way. It was strictly a matter of chance. If he opened one door, a fierce, hungry tiger would emerge and tear him to pieces, as punishment for his guilt. At the moment the criminal's fate was decided, doleful iron bells were clanged and great wails were heard from his mourners. Then the vast audience, with bowed heads and downcast hearts, slowly left for home.

However, if the accused subject opened the other door, a fair lady, the most suitable to his years and station that his majesty could find, came out into the arena. As a reward for his innocence, the accused was immediately married to her. It didn't matter if the subject was already married and had a family or if he already had a object for his affections, the king allowed no other arrangements to be made.

Another door would open beneath the king, and a priest, followed by a band of singers and dancing maidens blowing golden horns, came to where the pair stood, and the wedding was promptly solemnized. Gay brass bells rang out, the people shouted hurrahs, and the innocent man led his bride home.

This was the king's semi-barbaric way of administering justice. The accused criminal had no way of knowing out of which door the lady would come. Sometimes, she came out of the left door, at other times the right. The king considered this perfectly fair and determinate; the accused was instantly punished or rewarded. These public displays were very popular. The element of uncertainty added interest to the occasion. The masses were entertained. They didn't consider it unjust; after all, did not the accused have the entire matter in his own hands?

The king had a daughter, who was as strong-willed and whose soul was as fervent as his. He loved her beyond all others; she was the apple of his eye. She had a lover among the king's courtiers who was handsome and brave but of low station. She loved him with an ardor that was warm and strong. This love affair went on for several months until her father found out about it.

The king did not hesitate in what he considered his duty. He had the young man thrown into prison, and a day was set for his trial in the king's arena. This was an important occasion; no trial of this nature had happened before. The tiger cages of the kingdom were searched for the most savage beasts that could be found. The ranks of beautiful maidens were carefully surveyed to provide the young man with a suitable bride if chance did not determine otherwise.

Of course, everyone knew that the deed of which the young man had been accused had been done. He had loved the princess. The king would not think of allowing a fact like this to interfere with the working of the tribunal. In either case, the youth would be disposed of, and of course events would determine whether or not the young man had done wrong in allowing himself to love the princess.

The appointed day arrived. Attendance was so large that not everyone could fit into the arena. Crowds gathered outside the walls. The king and his court were in their places; all were ready. The signal was given, and the lover of the princess walked into the arena. His tall, handsome appearance was greeted with a hum of admiration. Most of the audience had not been aware that such a youth lived among them. No wonder the princess loved him!

As the youth entered the arena, he turned and bowed to the king; however, his eyes were fixed on the princess who sat to the right of her father. Had it not been for her strong-willed nature, she would probably have chosen not to be there. She had thought of nothing else since her father had put her lover in prison, however. She had to be there.

She had more power and influence than anyone previously connected with these tribunals. She was able to do what no one had been able to do before. She found out the secret of the doors. She knew behind which door was the cage of the tiger, and behind which stood the lady. Gold and the power of a woman's will had brought this information to her.

The princess not only knew behind which door the young lady would emerge, but she knew who the lady was. It was one of the fairest and loveliest damsels of the court who had been selected as reward for the accused youth, should he be proved innocent of the crime of aspiring to love one so far above him. The princess hated her. She had often seen, or imagined that she had seen, this fair creature casting glances of admiration upon her lover.

Occasionally, the princess thought that these glances were perceived and returned by the young man. She had seen the young woman and her lover have brief conversations. The girl was lovely, and she had dared to raise her eyes to the loved one of the princess. Partly due to the savage blood inherited from her father, the princess hated the woman who trembled behind the silent door.

When her lover looked at the princess, their eyes met as she sat in the arena, paler than anyone else in the crowd. He could tell that she knew behind which door crouched the tiger, and behind which stood the lady. Knowing her nature, he expected her to know. The young man knew that his only hope of certainty was based on the princess discovering the mystery. When he saw that she had succeeded, he knew that he would survive.

The young man's anxious glance asked the question, "Which?" It was as plain to her as if he had shouted the question. It was asked in a brief moment; it must be answered in another. Her right arm was positioned on the parapet in front of her. She raised her hand and made a slight, quick movement toward the right. No one but her lover saw her do it. All eyes were fixed on the man in the arena.

The young man turned and with a firm, rapid step walked across the arena. Every heart stopped beating, every breath was held, every eye was fixed on the man. Without hesitation, he went to the door on the right, and opened it. The point of this tale is this: Did the tiger come out of the door, or did the lady?

The question is difficult to answer because it involves a study of the human heart on the part of a hot-blooded, semi-barbaric princess. She had lost her lover, but would she allow someone that she hated to have him? Often, in her waking hours and in her dreams, she started in horror as she saw her lover open the door to the tiger. More often, she had seen him open the other door and gnashed her teeth as he saw his delight in greeting the lady. The princess's soul burned in agony as she saw him rush to meet the woman and the young woman's flushed cheeks and eyes sparkling with triumph.

Then, in her imagination, the princess heard the shouts of the multitude and heard the ringing of bells. She saw the priest advance to the couple and make them man and wife before her eyes. Then they walked away amid the cheering of the crowd, in which her one despairing shriek was drowned. Would it have been better for him to die at once and go to wait for her in the blessed region of the future? And yet, that awful tiger, those shrieks, that blood!

Her decision had been indicated in an instant, but had been made after days and nights of anguished deliberation. She had known that she would be asked. She had decided what she would answer. Without hesitation, had moved her hand to the right. The answer is left to the reader. Which came out of the opened door — the lady, or the tiger?

Moral: We have many choices in life. Sometimes lives rest on our decisions. Will we be selfless or self-serving?

Based on: Ralph L. Woods, "The Lady, or the Tiger,"
A Treasury of the Familiar

Tom Sawyer Gives Up the Brush

Saturday morning had come on the Mississippi River, and the summer world was bright, fresh, and brimming with life. There was a song in every heart, cheer in every face, and a spring in every step. The locust trees were in bloom and the fragrance of the blossoms filled the air. Cardiff Hill, beyond the village and above it, was green with vegetation, and it lay just far enough away to seem dreamy, reposeful, and inviting.

Tom Sawyer appeared on the sidewalk with a bucket of whitewash and a long-handled brush. He surveyed the fence, and all gladness left him; a deep melancholy settled upon his spirit. Thirty yards of fence nine feet high. Life seemed to him hollow, and existence a burden. Sighing, he dipped his brush and moved it along the top plank; he repeated the process and did it again. He compared the insignificant whitewashed streak with the far-reaching expanse of unwhitewashed fence and sat down on a box discouraged.

Soon the carefree boys would come tripping along on all sorts of delicious expeditions, and they would make fun of him for having to work. The thought of it burned him like fire. He got out his worldly wealth and examined it—bits of toys, marbles, and trash; enough to buy an exchange of work, maybe, but not half enough to buy so much as a half-hour of freedom. So he returned his possessions to his pocket and gave up on the idea of trying to buy the boys. At this dark and hopeless moment an inspiration burst upon him! It was nothing less than a great, magnificent inspiration.

Tom picked up his brush and went to work. Ben Rogers came into sight presently—the very boy, of all boys, whose ridicule Tom had been dreading. Ben's gait was the hop-skip-and-jump—proof that his heart was light and his anticipations high. He was eating an apple and making the sounds of his personal imitation of a steamboat. As he drew near, he slackened speed, took the middle of the street, leaned far over to starboard and rounded to ponderously and with laborious pomp and circumstance—for he was impersonating the *Big Missouri* and considering himself to be drawing nine feet of water. He was boat captain and engine bells combined, so he had to imagine himself standing on his own hurricane deck giving orders and executing them.

Tom went on whitewashing. He paid no attention to the steamboat. Ben stared a moment and then said, "Hi! You're a stump, aren't you!" No answer. Tom surveyed his last touch with the eye of an artist; then he gave his brush another gentle sweep and surveyed the result, as before. Ben came up alongside of him. Tom's mouth watered for the apple, but he stuck to his work. Ben said, "Hello, old chap, you've got to work, hey?"

Tom turned suddenly and said. "Why, it's you, Ben! I wasn't noticing."

"Say—I'm going swimming, I am. Don't you wish you could? But of course you'd rather work—wouldn't you? Of course you would!"

Tom contemplated the boy and said, "What do you call work?"

"Why, isn't that work?"

Tom resumed whitewashing and answered carelessly, "Well, maybe it is, and maybe it isn't. All I know is, it suits Tom Sawyer."

"Oh come, now, you don't mean that you like it?"

The brush continued to move. "Like it? Well, I don't see why I shouldn't like it. Does a boy get a chance to whitewash a fence every day?"

That put things in a new light. Ben stopped nibbling his apple. Tom swept the brush gently back and forth—stepped back to note the effect—added a touch here and there—critically scanned the effect again—Ben watching every move and getting more and more interested, more and more absorbed.

Presently he said, "Say, Tom, let me whitewash a little."

Tom considered and was about to consent, but he changed his mind:

"No—no—I reckon it wouldn't do, Ben. You see, Aunt Polly's awful particular about this fence—right here on the street, you know—but if it was the back fence I wouldn't mind and she wouldn't. Yes, she's awful particular about this fence; it's got to be done very carefully. I reckon there isn't one boy in a thousand, maybe two thousand, that can do it the way it's got to be done."

"No—is that so? Oh come, now—let me just try. Only just a little—I'd let you, if you were me, Tom."

"Ben, I'd like to; but Aunt Polly—well, Jim wanted to do it, but she wouldn't let him; Sid wanted to do it, and she wouldn't let Sid. Now don't you see how I'm fixed? If you were to tackle this fence and anything was to happen to it—"

"Oh, I'll be just as careful. Now let me try. Say—I'll give you the core of my apple."

"Well, there—No, Ben, now don't. I'm afraid—"

"I'll give you all of it."

Tom gave up the brush with reluctance in his face, but eagerness in his heart. And as the steamer *Big Missouri* worked and sweated in the sun, the retired artist sat on a barrel in the shade nearby, dangled his legs, munched his apple, and planned the slaughter of more innocents. There was no lack of material. Boys happened along every little while. They came to jeer, but stayed to whitewash. By the time Ben was tired, Tom traded the next chance to Billy Fisher for a kite, in good repair. When he played out, Johnny Miller bought in for twelve marbles—and so on, hour after hour.

When the middle of the afternoon came, from being a poverty-stricken boy in the morning, Tom was literally rolling in wealth.

Besides the things already mentioned, he had a piece of blue bottle glass, a key that wouldn't unlock anything, a piece of chalk, a glass stopper, a tin soldier, six firecrackers, a brass doorknob, a dog collar, the handle of a knife, and an old window sash.

Tom had a nice, idle time all the while with plenty of company—and the fence had three coats of whitewash. If he hadn't run out of whitewash, he would have bankrupted every boy in the village.

Tom admitted to himself that it wasn't such a hollow world, after all. He had discovered a great law of human action, without knowing it—namely that in order to make a man or boy covet a thing, it is necessary only to make the thing difficult to obtain. If he had been a great and wise philosopher, he would now have comprehended that Work consists of whatever one is obliged to do, and that Play consists of whatever one is not obliged to do.

This helped Tom understand why constructing artificial flowers or performing on a treadmill is work, while bowling or climbing Mont Blanc is only amusement. Tom mused awhile over the substantial change that had taken place in his worldly circumstances, and then went into headquarters to report to Aunt Polly.

Moral: Shrewdness and cleverness accomplish more than coercion. What is apparently unobtainable is the most desirable.

Based on: Mark Twain, "Tom Sawyer Gives Up the Brush," *The Adventures of Tom Sawyer*

The Last Leaf

Just west of Washington Square in New York City, the streets have broken themselves into small strips called "places." These "places" make strange angles and curves. So, to quaint old Greenwich Village the art people soon came prowling, hunting for north windows, eighteenth-century gables, Dutch attics, and low rents.

At the top of a squatty, three-story brick building, Sue and Johnsy had their studio. "Johnsy" was a nickname for Joanna. They had met at an inexpensive restaurant on Eighth Street and found that their tastes in art and chicory salad were so congenial that the joint studio resulted.

That was in May. In November a cold, unseen stranger, whom doctors called pneumonia, stalked the village, touched one here and one there. Over on the east side this ravager strode boldly, smiting victims by the scores, but trod slowly through the maze of the narrow "places." Pneumonia smote Johnsy; and she lay, scarcely moving on her painted iron bedstead, looking through the Dutch windowpanes at the blank side of the next brick house.

One morning the busy doctor had a frown on his brow when he invited Sue into the hallway and told her: "She has one chance in— let us say, ten, and that chance is for her to want to live. The way people have of lining up on the side of the undertaker makes the entire pharmacy manual look silly. Your little lady has made up her mind that she's not going to get well. Has she anything on her mind?"

"She wanted to paint the Bay of Naples someday," said Sue.

The doctor was surprised at this and asked if she had anything worth thinking about on her mind—a man, for instance.

Sue acknowledged that there was no man in her life.

The doctor said, "Well, it is the weakness, then. I will do all that science, so far as it may filter through my efforts, can accomplish. If you will get her to ask one question about the new winter styles, I will promise you a one-in-five chance for her instead of one-in-ten."

After the doctor left, Sue went into the workroom and cried her eyes out. Then she swaggered into Johnsy's room with her drawing board, whistling a ragtime tune.

Johnsy lay with her face toward the window. Sue stopped whistling, thinking that she was asleep. She moved to the bedside and saw that Johnsy's eyes were wide open. She was looking out of the window and counting—counting backward. "Twelve," she said, and a little later "eleven," and then "ten," and "nine," and then "eight" and "seven," almost together.

Sue looked out of the window and wondered what there was to count. There was only a bare, dreary yard to be seen, and the blank side of the brick house twenty feet away. An old ivy vine, gnarled and decayed at the roots, climbed halfway up the brick wall. The cold wind of autumn had stricken its leaves from the vine until its skeleton branches clung, almost bare, to the crumbling bricks. Sue asked Johnsy what she was looking at.

"Six," said Johnsy, in a whisper. "They're falling faster now. Three days ago there were almost a hundred. It made my head ache to count them. But now it's easy. There goes another one. There are only five left now."

Sue said, "Five what, tell me."

"Leaves on the ivy vine. When the last one falls I must go too."

"I've never heard of such nonsense," complained Sue, with scorn. "What have old ivy leaves have to do with your getting well? And you used to love that vine. Why, the doctor told me this morning that your chances for getting well real soon were ten to one! Try to have some broth now, and let me get back to my drawing."

Johnsy kept her eyes fixed out the window. "There goes another. No, I don't want any broth. That leaves just four. I want to see the last one fall before it gets dark. Then I'll go, too."

Sue asked, "Johnsy, will you promise me to keep your eyes closed and not look out the window until I am done working? I must hand this drawing in by tomorrow. I need the light or I would draw with the shades down."

Johnsy asked why Sue didn't draw in the other room and was told that she wanted to be with her and didn't want her looking at those silly ivy leaves.

Johnsy closed her eyes and said, "Tell me as soon as you are finished because I want to see the last one fall. I'm tired of waiting. I'm tired of thinking. I want to turn loose my hold on everything, and go sailing down, down, like one of those poor, tired leaves."

"Try to sleep," said Sue. "I must call Behrman up to model for my drawing. I won't be gone long."

Old Behrman was a painter who lived on the ground floor of their building. He was over sixty and had a long beard and the body of an imp. Behrman was a failure in art. He had wielded the brush for forty years and had been always about to paint a masterpiece, but he had never begun it. He painted some commercial and advertising art to earn a living. He also served as a model to those young artists in the village who could not afford a professional. He drank too much gin and talked of his coming masterpiece.

Behrman was a fierce little old man who scoffed at softness in anyone, and who considered himself a special guardian to the two young artists in the studio above. Sue found him smelling strongly of juniper berries in his dimly lit work area below. In the corner was a blank canvas on an easel, waiting to receive the first strokes of a masterpiece. She told him about Johnsy's fancy and how she feared that Johnsy would, light and fragile as a leaf herself, float away when her slight hold on the world grew weaker.

Old Behrman spoke contemptuously of such idiotic imaginings. He was amazed that there were people in the world foolish enough to die because leaves drop off from a confounded vine. He had never heard of such a thing. He asked Sue why she would allow such silly business to enter Johnsy's head. Sue said, "She is very ill and weak, and the fever has left her mind morbid and full of strange fancies."

Johnsy was sleeping when Behrman came upstairs with Sue to pose for her. Sue pulled the shade down to the window sill and motioned Behrman into the other room. They peered out the window at the ivy vine. They looked at each other for a moment without speaking. A persistent, cold rain was falling, mingled with snow. Behrman took his place on a stool to model for Sue's drawing.

When Sue awoke the next morning she found Johnsy with dull, wide-open eyes staring at the drawn window shade. Johnsy ordered, "Pull it up; I want to see." Wearily Sue obeyed. Even after the beating rain and fierce gusts of wind throughout the night, one ivy leaf stood out against the brick wall. It was the last one on the vine. Still dark near its stem, but with its serrated edges tinted with the yellow of decay, it hung bravely from a branch twenty feet above the ground.

Johnsy said, "It is the last one. I thought it would surely fall during the night. I heard the wind. It will fall today, and I shall die at the same time."

Sue said, "Think of me, if you won't think of yourself. What would I do?" Johnsy did not answer. The lonesomest thing in the world is a soul when it is making ready to go on its mysterious far journey. The fancy seemed to possess her more strongly as one by one the ties that bound her to friendship and to earth were loosened.

The day wore on until even in the twilight they could see the lone ivy leaf clinging to its stem against the wall. Then with the coming of the night the north wind began to blow again, and the rain beat against the windows and poured down from the low Dutch eaves. When it was daylight, Johnsy commanded that the shade be raised. The ivy leaf was still there. Johnsy looked at it for a long time, then she called to Sue, who was preparing more chicken broth.

Johnsy said, "I've been a bad girl, Sue. Something has made that last leaf stay there to show me how wicked I was. It was a sin to want to die. You may bring me some chicken broth now and also bring me a hand mirror and pack some pillows around me so I can watch you cook." Later Johnsy said, "Sue, some day I really hope to paint the Bay of Naples."

The doctor came in the afternoon and told Sue that Johnsy's chances for survival were even and that good nursing would tip the scale in her favor. As he was leaving, the doctor told Sue that he had another case downstairs. "Behrman his name is—some kind of artist, I believe. Pneumonia, too. He is an old, weak man and the attack is acute. There is no hope for him; he is going to the hospital today to be made more comfortable."

The next day the doctor told Sue that her patient was out of danger. He recommended good nutrition and good care. That afternoon Sue went in to see Johnsy who was knitting a scarf. Sue put her arms around her and said that she had something to tell her.

"Mr. Behrman died of pneumonia today in the hospital. He was ill only two days. The janitor found him on the morning of the first day in his room helpless with pain. His shoes and clothing were wet through and icy cold. They couldn't imagine where he had been on such a dreadful night. And then they found a lantern, still lighted, and a ladder that had been dragged from its place, and some scattered brushes, and a palette with green and yellow colors mixed on it, and—look out the window at the last ivy leaf on the wall. Didn't you wonder why it never fluttered or moved when the wind blew? It's Behrman's masterpiece—he painted it there the night that the last leaf fell."

Moral: One of life's greatest accomplishments is doing things for others.

Based on: O. Henry, "The Last Leaf," *Tales of O. Henry*

Epilogue

The ultimate value of great legends lies in their inspiring poetry,
Their moral values and their attitude to life.
It is poetically right for the blinded Samson to bring down
The pillars of the Philistine temple upon his enemies and himself,
For Robert Bruce to learn a lesson in resolution from the spider,
For Roland in his obdurate pride to sound the great horn too late
    at Rencesvals,
For the glory of Arthur and his champions of the Round Table
To end in betrayal, destruction and bitter grief.
In legend courage, loyalty, generosity, and greatness of heart
Are upheld against cowardice, treachery, meanness and
    poorness of spirit.
The lesson which the supreme heroes of legend and history have
    to teach is that life need not be petty,
That existence can be vivid, exciting, and intense,
That the limits of human reach and achievement are
Not as narrow and restricted as they so often seem.

Richard Cavendish, *Legends of the World*

Notes

Many of these legends and tales have been passed down by story-tellers and have evolved in the telling. The author gratefully acknowledges the works of other authors, including those from earlier eras, such as James Baldwin (1841-1925), Jesse Lyman Hurlbut (1843-1930), and Andrew Lang (1844-1912), who preserved our heritage and whose endeavors provided many of the stories presented here. These legends and tales have been rewritten to provide a consistent writing style.

Vector art is from IMSI's MasterClips Collection, 1895 Francisco Blvd. East, San Rafael, CA 94901-5506, USA

Bibliography

Baldwin, James. *Favorite Tales of Long Ago*. New York:
E. P. Dutton, 1955.

—. *Fifty Famous People: A Book of Short Stories*. New York:
American Book, 1912.

—. *Fifty Famous Stories Retold*. New York: American Book,
1896.

Barnard, Mary. *The Mythmakers*. Athens, Ohio:
Ohio University Press, 1966.

Becquer, Gustavo Adolfo. *Romantic Legends of Spain*.
New York: Thomas Y. Crowell, 1909.

Bennett, William, ed. *The Book of Virtues*. New York:
Simon & Schuster, 1993.

The Holy Bible. New York: The Douay Bible House, 1945.

Bierlein, J. F. *Parallel Myths*. New York: Ballantine Books, 1994.

Bulfinch, Thomas. *Bulfinch's Mythology*. London: Spring Books,
1967.

Calvino, Italo, ed. *Italian Folktales*. New York:
Harcourt Brace Jovanovich, 1956.

Cavendish, Richard. *Legends of the World*. New York:
Schocken Books, 1982.

Clouston, W. A. *Popular Tales and Fictions, vol. 2*. Edinburgh:
William Blackwood, 1887.

Coffin, Tristam Potter, and Hennig Cohen, eds.
The Parade of Heroes: Legendary Figures in American Lore.
Garden City: Doubleday, 1978.

Colum, Padraic. *Orpheus: Myths of the World*. New York:
Macmillan, 1930.

Cruse, Amy. *The Book of Myths*. New York: Gramercy Books,
1993.

De Maupassant, Guy. *The Best Stories of Guy De Maupassant*.
New York: Modern Library, 1945.

Eliot, Alexander. *The Global Myths: Exploring Primitive, Pagan,
Sacred, and Scientific Mythologies*. New York: Continuum,
1993.

Esenwein, J. Berg, and Marietta Stockard. *Children's Stories and
How to Tell Them*. Springfield, MA:
Home Correspondence School, 1919.

Gibson, Katherine. *The Golden Bird and Other Stories.*
New York: Macmillan, 1927.

Goodrich, Norma Lorre. *Myths of the Hero.* New York:
Orion Press, 1958.

Grossman, David. Lion's Honey: *The Myth of Samson.*
Edinburgh: Canongate, 2006.

Harrell, John and Mary, eds. *A Storyteller's Treasury.* New York:
Harcourt, 1977.

Hawthorne, Nathaniel. *The Wonder Book.* New York:
Franklin Watts, 1963.

Henry, O. *The Complete Edition of O. Henry.* Garden City:
Doubleday, 1906.

Hodgetts, Edith M. S. *Tales and Legends from the Land of the
Tzar.* London: Griffith Farran, 1891.

Hubbard, Elbert. *A Message to Garcia and Other Essays.*
New York: Crowell, 1917.

Hurlbut, Jesse Lyman. *Hurlbut's Story of the Bible for the Young
and Old.* New York: Holt, 1957.

Irving, Washington. *The Alhambra: Tales and Sketches of the
Moors and Spaniards.* New York: A. L. Burt, 1924.

Jenkins, Elizabeth. *The Mystery of King Arthur.* New York:
Coward, McCann & Geoghegan, 1975.

Klees, Emerson. *More Legends and Stories of the Finger Lakes
Region.* Rochester, NY: Friends of the Finger Lakes
Publishing, 1997.

Lang, Andrew. *The Book of Romance.* London:
Longmans, Green, 1902.

—. *Lilac Fairy Book.* New York: Dover, 1968.

—. *Pink Fairy Book.* New York: Dover, 1967.

Macmillan, Cyrus. *Canadian Wonder Tales.* London: John Lane,
1918.

Mallory, Sir Thomas. *Le Morte d'Arthur.* New York:
Bramhall House, 1962.

Monro, H. H. *Complete Short Stories of Saki.* New York:
Simon and Schuster, 1947.

Muller-Guggenbuhl, Fritz. *Swiss-Alpine Folktales.* London:
Oxford University Press, 1964.

Rugoff, Milton, ed. *A Harvest of World Folk Tales.* New York:
Viking, 1949.

Ruiz, Mario and Jerry A. Novick. *Samson: Judge of Israel.*
New York: Metron Press, 2002.

Tolstoy, Leo. *How Much Land Does a Man Need? and Other
Stories.* New York: Penguin Books, 1993.

—. *Walk in the Light and Twenty-three Tales.* Boston:
Plough Publishing, 1998.

Twain, Mark. *The Adventures of Tom Sawyer.* New York:
Harper & Brothers, 1903.

Woods, Ralph L., ed. *A Treasury of the Familiar.* New York:
Macmillan, 1943.

Yonge, Charlotte Mary. *A Book of Golden Deeds of All Times
and All Lands.* London: Macmillan, 1866.